From the Files of

Madison Finn

Read all the books about Madison Finn!

Coming Soon!

From the Files of
Madison Finn

Picture-Perfect

By Laura Dower

HYPERION
New York

Text copyright © 2002 by Laura Dower

From the Files of Madison Finn, Volo, and the Volo colophon are trademarks of Disney Enterprises, Inc.

Printed in the United States of America

First Edition
5 7 9 10 8 6

The main body of text of this book is set in 13-point Frutiger Roman.

ISBN 0-7868-1682-1

Visit www.madisonfinn.com

For Liisa, fashion diva and my BFF

"You have the new issue of *Teen Blast*!" Madison said, grabbing the magazine off her friend Fiona Waters's bed. On the cover was Nikki, the most popular pop star all over Far Hills Junior High—and across the globe.

"Oh my God! Isn't she beeee-yootiful?" Madison's other friend Aimee Gillespie said, reaching for the magazine from Madison. "I wish I looked just like this."

In the cover photo, Nikki was wearing a tube top, shorts, and glitter makeup. Neon blue streaks striped her hair, and she had on three-inch platform shoes.

"Sure, Aim," Madison said, laughing. "I can just see you painting your hair that color. And those shoes would look good in ballet class."

Fiona giggled. "Read the article, you two. It says that she's dating one of the guys from Jimmy J."

"That's a lie!" Aimee said. "Let me see."

The three friends plopped down onto the carpeted floor in Fiona's bedroom and flipped to the cover story: "Meet Nikki Up Close!" There was a photographic spread with Nikki in different costumes, including some shots from her last concert.

"I love that outfit," Fiona said, pointing to a cropped silver shirt.

"She has a ring on every finger. Just like me," Madison said.

"Nikki was born near Far Hills?" Aimee said, reading the text of the article aloud. "Wow. She is like us. Did you know she lived near here?"

Fiona nodded. "Of course I knew that."

"How could you not have known that?" Madison asked Aimee.

"I don't know," Aimee shrugged. "I'm not a Nikki expert or anything. Geesh."

"Nikki has the perfect life," Fiona mused. "She's visited something like fifty countries. How cool is that?"

Madison nodded. "She has a movie coming out, too, I think."

"She really has perfect hair," Aimee moaned.

"You have hair like Nikki's, Aimee," Fiona said.

"Nah, mine isn't as blond as hers. She has a better haircut. And look at her stomach. It is soooo flat."

"You can say that again," Madison said. "I wish I had her stomach. I wish I had her whole body."

"What?" Fiona asked. "What's wrong with your body, Maddie?"

"You mean besides my butt?" Madison chuckled.

"What are you talking about?" Fiona said.

Madison sighed. "Come on, Fiona. Nikki is perfect and . . . well . . . I'm not exactly . . ."

"Maddie!" Fiona cried. "You guys need a reality check. She is not perfect. My dad told me that there are artists who airbrush pictures of celebrities like Nikki so that they look perfect. No one is *that* perfect."

"I thought you liked her," Madison said.

"I do," Fiona said. "I like her clothes and her songs and her cool life—"

"Come on, Fiona," Aimee grumbled. "We're all just jealous. Admit it."

"What*ever*!" Fiona threw her arms into the air and got up off the floor. "I'm going to get something to drink. Does anyone else want a snack?"

"Um, did your mom make any cookies today?" Madison asked coyly.

Fiona's mother, Mrs. Waters, was the Cookie Queen. She baked baskets of gingersnaps and sugar wafers when Fiona and her twin brother Chet had friends over to visit.

"Maddie!" Aimee nudged Madison with her elbow. "How can you eat cookies? You just said you wished you were more like Nikki. Do you think she

3

eats cookies all day? You can't eat that stuff if you want people to notice you."

"What are you talking about? What *people*?" Madison said.

"People at school," Aimee said. "You know. Guys. *Everyone*."

"But I like cookies," Madison said.

"I like cookies, too, Maddie," Fiona said. "I'll go see if Mom made any."

Fiona disappeared toward the kitchen to get a tray of snacks, leaving Madison and Aimee alone in her bedroom.

Aimee stood up and walked over to Fiona's bulletin board. It was decorated with photographs, postcards, and a row of colored ribbons Fiona had won over the years playing sports. There was a spring soccer schedule tacked up on the board, too, with dates of upcoming matches.

"No wonder Fiona doesn't stress about her stomach," Aimee said. "She's always playing soccer."

"Well," Madison said. "You do ballet every day."

"*Almost* every day," Aimee said. "It's not the same."

Madison dropped onto Fiona's bed and bounced lightly. "Let's hear some tunes," she said, pointing to the digital clock radio on Fiona's nightstand.

Aimee clicked it on and surfed for a station they liked. A high-pitched voice sang a familiar melody.

4

And I know
Yes, I do
From the moment we met
Yes, us two

"Oh my God!" Aimee squealed. "It's NIKKI!"

"Turn it up," Madison yelled.

The two girls bounced on and off the edge of Fiona's bed, singing every lyric along with the radio.

I wanna be closer still
There's a place in my heart that you fill
I could be what you want
I know this is true

Aimee leaped up and twirled around, striking a pose as if she were singing into a microphone.

Madison fell backward onto the bed, laughing.

"What are you guys doing?" Fiona asked, walking back into the room with a tray of juice boxes and chocolate-chip cookies.

"Nikki's on the radio!" Aimee said, still dancing.

I could be sugar-sweet like you
Sugar, sugar-sweet

Fiona smiled. She put the tray down on her nightstand, and the three friends joined together in a circle.

5

"SUGAR-SWEET!" they squealed as the last chorus ended and Nikki's voice faded away.

"This is Stevie Steves and you're listening to WKBM KABOOM! Far Hills radio," the announcer's voice roared across the airwaves once the song had finished. "And that was sugar-sweet superstar Nikki performing her number-one smash hit 'Sugar Sweet Like You.'"

"I LOVE that song!" Madison said.

The announcer continued. "But that's not all, listeners. Get this! Nikki is coming to Far Hills. Stay tuned for details. . . ."

Madison, Aimee, and Fiona stopped short, jaws open.

"Did he just say—?" Madison gasped.

"Oh my God!" Aimee said.

Fiona sat down on the edge of her bed near the radio. "Shh! Shh! Let's listen and hear what they have to say!"

As the radio commercial finished, Stevie Steves came back onto the radio. "Tune in to win tickets to Nikki right here!"

"SHE'S COMING TO FAR HILLS?" Aimee screeched. "WE CAN WIN?"

"Shh!" Fiona hushed. "My mom will hear us."

Aimee couldn't contain her excitement. She continued to jump around the room.

Knock-knock.

The three friends looked at each other, sure that

Mrs. Waters had heard. Fiona went to open the door, but Chet poked his head inside before she could get there.

"Keep it down in there!" Chet barked. "Quit screaming."

"Get out of my room, dork!" Fiona snapped back, throwing a shoe at the door.

"You're the dork!" Chet shot back, slamming the door behind him.

Madison and Aimee just laughed.

"I'm glad I don't have a brother," Madison said, grabbing a cookie.

Aimee put her hands on her hips. "Yeah, and I have *three*. Lucky me."

Fiona stuffed a cookie in her mouth too, but Aimee said she didn't want one. "How can you guys eat at a time like this? We have a chance to win tickets to a Nikki concert!"

Madison took another bite. "Mmmmmmm?"

"What does that have to do with anything, Aim?" Fiona said.

The radio announcer came back on with all the contest details. "To win, all you need to do is to call us here at WKBM KABOOM! And if you're the lucky random caller, you may be chosen as a super Nikki ticket winner. That means four tickets for you and your closet friends—plus a special trip backstage to meet Nikki up close!"

"Meet Nikki!" Aimee squealed. "Oh my God!"

"We could *all* go!" Madison said. "This is so exciting!"

"Okay, I'm going to call," Fiona said, turning down the volume on the radio and picking up the phone receiver.

Fiona had her very own phone right there in her bedroom. It was the coolest shade of grape-purple, and Madison loved the rainbow stickers she'd used to decorate the handle.

"Call NOW!" Stevie Steves said.

Fiona dialed the number for WKBM.

"Oh, it's busy," Fiona growled, hanging up and dialing again. Luckily, her phone had a redial button.

But it was still busy.

"Keep trying," Aimee insisted. "Keep trying."

Knock-knock.

Chet poked his head in the door.

"What do you want?" Fiona yelled.

"Are you on the phone or what? I want to use it," Chet said. "You can't hog it all the time."

Fiona put her hands on her hips. "You have to wait. I'm using it right now."

Madison and Aimee giggled.

"What are you dorks laughing about?" Chet asked, glaring at them.

"GET OUT OF MY ROOM, CHET!" Fiona screeched again.

"If you're not off the phone soon, I'm telling Mom," Chet threatened.

Fiona snarled. "Fine," as Chet walked out in a huff, slamming the door behind him.

Without missing a beat, Fiona picked up the phone and dialed the radio station once again. Still busy. She tried for at least five minutes as Madison and Aimee watched. After hitting redial about a hundred times more, Fiona's eyes grew wide.

"It's ringing!" she squealed, pressing her ear to the receiver. "It's ringing!"

Madison and Aimee leaned in close to see what would happen.

"Did they answer?" Aimee asked.

"Shhh!" Fiona said. Her eyes got even wider. "Hello?"

Madison could hear soft voices on the radio in the background, so she went over to listen. Stevie Steves was about to talk to his tenth random ticket winner of the day.

Aimee covered her mouth with her palms so she wouldn't scream.

"Hello?" Fiona said again. "Yes, I was calling to win Nikki tickets."

She looked like she was about to faint.

"What are they saying? What are they saying?" Aimee asked. She started bouncing on the bed again.

"I WON?" Fiona screeched. "Oh, sorry about that," she apologized to the person on the other end of the phone. "I didn't mean to scream,

9

but did I really and truly win tickets to the concert?"

Fiona listened closely, cheeks flushed. She gave the phone operator her name and then they put her on hold.

"They want me to wait," Fiona blurted to Madison and Aimee. "They said I'm gonna be on the radio in a few minutes. With Stevie Steves!"

The three friends let out an enormous squeal. Fiona almost dropped the phone.

Madison couldn't turn up the radio to hear because that would cause feedback, so she and Aimee leaned in close while Fiona talked on the phone on the other side of the bedroom.

"This is Stevie Steves back again with the winner of the hour," the announcer said. "We have Fiona on the line. Fiona, are you there?"

Fiona froze. She said nothing.

"Fiona, are you there?" Stevie Steves asked again.

Madison and Aimee shot a look in Fiona's direction, which snapped Fiona out of her overexcited trance.

"I'm here," she blurted. "Did I win?"

"You betcha," Stevie Steves said. "So tell me, are you a Nikki fan?"

Before Fiona could even answer, Aimee let out another squeak. Madison did too. Fiona joined in. The announcer heard it all.

"So, you're there with friends?" the announcer asked, chuckling to himself. "Either that or we've got some very large mice in the background there."

"We're all the hugest fans of Nikki in the whole world," Fiona gushed. "The *hugest*. Absolutely."

"Well, you and your friends have won tickets to Nikki's exclusive Far Hills concert in two weeks. Stay on the line and our operator will get all your information," he explained. "And listeners, you should stay tuned to WKBM for more great music in the coming hour."

Fiona gave the switchboard at the station her information and hung up the phone. They would have to call back and confirm the win with a parent, since Fiona was under sixteen.

"This is so awesome," Aimee said. "I'm shaking."

"Nobody ever wins tickets," Madison said, hugging Fiona tightly around the waist. "I can't believe you won!"

"We all won," Fiona said, grinning from ear to ear. "And now we're going to our very first concert together."

 Nikki

Life is so unfair.

No, Fiona's mother is the one who is sooo unfair.

Today after school, the radio station called Fiona's house to say that YES we'd won the tickets to the Nikki concert and could we get parental approval? It's some legal thing since we're not sixteen. N e way, Mrs. Waters almost <u>hung up on them</u>! She asked them a zillion dumb questions and Fiona was so embarrassed. We all were. Then Mrs. Waters got madder than mad at Fiona for calling WKBM on the phone so much, especially on a school night. She thought we'd been hanging in Fiona's room doing homework or something.

I think Chet ratted. Geek

Mrs. Waters thinks we're all too young to go to a concert. THAT IS SO UNFAIR! I really, really hope my mom turns out to be cool about this. WE HAVE TO GO! This is a once-in-a-lifetime opportunity.

I hope Aimee has already asked her mom and she is okay w/the idea. If Mrs. Gillespie doesn't think we should go then we're TOTALLY doomed. Mom will probably cave in and do whatever Mrs. Gillespie and the other mothers want to do. Help! I wish there were a way we could convince our parents to let us go.

Rude awakening: Life is what happens when you're busy making other plans. Unfortunately, it's the life that MOMS make up all the rules for.

Ugh.

"Madison! Are you up there?" Mom yelled.

Madison got up from her desk and went to the doorway. "What?" she hollered back.

"I just wanted to tell you that your dad called," Mom said.

"When?" Madison asked.

"About an hour ago. He's still away on business."

Madison let out an enormous sigh. "I was here, Mom. I didn't hear the phone ring. Why didn't you get me?"

"I was on the line with Paul when it beeped," Mom explained, a wide smile growing across her face.

13

"Oh," Madison said. The lovey-dovey look on Mom's face made Madison squirm.

Mom had just started dating Paul, a coworker from Budge Films. Madison didn't want to hear any of the gory "date" details. It was hard enough getting used to divorced parents on their own, let alone dealing with their brand-new significant others. Dad had been dating Stephanie for a while, and Madison still struggled with the idea of his having a girlfriend. Facing Mom's love life was even worse.

"So how's Paul?" Madison said, trying to be nice.

"He's fine," Mom said. "And he says hello, by the way. Contrary to popular opinion, Paul thinks that you're a good kid. Imagine that?"

"Ha-ha. Very funny, Mom," Madison said, grinning. "Well, say hello back, I guess."

"I will," Mom said, winking. "Now go send your dad an e-mail or something. He said he'd try calling back again later, too."

Madison turned on her heel and headed back to her laptop.

Paul shmall.

What was the big deal about this film-editor guy anyway? Madison didn't really like the way Paul's name sounded. She also didn't like the fact that Mom kept talking to him when Dad was on the phone.

Everything was SO unfair.

Once upstairs, Madison sat down to send Dad the quick e-mail. Online was the way they communicated best. Dad was the first person who had shown Madison how to use a computer; and he was always finding new Internet tricks and shortcuts to share. He sent her e-mails every other day, too.

Madison logged onto bigfishbowl.com and punched in her password. Then she headed into her e-mailbox, and clicked on NEW.

```
From: MadFinn
To: JeffFinn
Subject: Hellooooo
Date: Thurs 16 May 6:04 PM
```

Mom said you called but she was on the phone with you-know-who. How are things? I'm sad we couldn't have dinner tonight like we planned, but I understand things come up. You said the meeting might go a day or two longer than you expected so that's cool.

I have a question 4 u: what's your opinion of kids going to concerts? I mean, if I wanted to go to a concert, for example, would you let me go? What if it were a really mellow concert with other kids? I mean, other GOOD kids.

I think you'll say it sounds great, but I wanted to double-check just to be sure.

You would say yes, right?

By the way, I miss you bunches.

Madison punched SEND. After the Dad mail was sent, Madison saw that she had new e-mails.

```
FROM                SUBJECT
⊠ BeAllYouCanBe99  Magic! Never Feel Fat Again!
⊠ FHASC            Clinic Update: Super-Collies
⊠ Wetwinz          Concert
⊠ BalletGrl        Fw: Re: Concert
```

Madison scanned the list. There was only one name she didn't recognize: BeAllYouCanBe99. It turned out to be an ad for special weight-loss powder. Madison wondered why *she* was getting something like that.

DELETE.

She also picked up e-mail from the Far Hills Animal Shelter and Clinic (FHASC). The clinic had begun to send weekly updates on activities and pets. Madison had been volunteering there on and off in seventh grade. The newsletters told "success stories" of sad animals that had been happily adopted. Today, Madison read about the miraculous animal rescue of two collies that had been trapped in a fire. Madison knew those collies: Mutt and Jeff. She had pulled their photos from the newsletter and saved them as screen savers.

"Yikes!" Madison said as her eyes caught the digital clock in the corner of her laptop screen. It was after six o'clock, and she still had two e-mails from her BFFs left to read. Each was marked with a giant exclamation point for "high priority."

```
From:  Wetwinz
To: MadFinn; BalletGrl
Subject: Concert
Date: Thurs 16 May 6:04 PM
Hello? I tried calling your house,
Maddie, but it just rang and rang.
Is ur call-waiting working? Aimee,
ur brother Dean told me he'd give u
the message but u haven't called
yet. WHERE R U GUYS????

My dad isn't home yet from this big
mtg 2day so I still dunno if we can
go 2 the concert or not. My mother
sez she wants to talk 2 Daddy first
& then she wants to call ur moms.
What did they say when U asked
about the concert? I am so afraid
this won't happen now. WBS!!!
```

Aimee had sent an e-mail reply back to both friends.

From: BalletGrl
To: Wetwinz; MadFinn
Subject: Fw: Re: Concert
Date: Thurs 16 May 6:21 PM

Dean never said n e thing about you calling?! I NEVER got a message, Fiona. NEVER.

No, I haven't talked to Mom either. She's in a really crabby mood tonight so I'm sorta avoiding her. Today Blossom my dog got into some white paint and made a huge mess on the floor and on her fur. Mom is soooo mad. I know if I asked her tonight about the concert she'd say NO way. She gets like that sometimes—super strict.

p.s. I just got an e-mail from my dance teacher and I was chosen to do a small solo piece in the spring revue. Isn't that amazing?
p.p.s. Maddie, what did ur mom say about the concert?

Madison sighed.
Aimee hadn't spoken to *her* mom.
Madison hadn't spoken to *her* mom.
And Fiona's mom was being weird about the whole thing.

The trio was inches away from losing their four free tickets. What could Madison do to help their situation?

What would Bigwheels do?

Bigwheels was Madison's keypal, good at dishing out online advice in difficult situations just like this one. Madison moved into the chat rooms on Bigfishbowl.com to see if maybe Bigwheels was online. She could help right now if she were there.

Luckily, Madison found Bigwheels right away. She was hiding out inside a Math Homework chat room called "GEOMETRY."

```
<MadFinn>: Bigwheels? Can u talk?
<Bigwheels>: RN!
<MadFinn>: r u @ school?
<Bigwheels>: Did I tell u I was in
    math club?
```

The most interesting part about having a keypal who lived all the way across the country was the surprises. Madison was learning new things about her online friend every time they spoke.

```
<MadFinn>: if ur busy I don't wanna
    bug u
<Bigwheels>: im in the lab after
    school but I can talk
<MadFinn>: do u like Nikki
<Bigwheels>: #1 fan
```

```
<MadFinn>: well we won tix to her
   concert
<Bigwheels>: get out!
<MadFinn>: imserious
<Bigwheels>: YTTT?
<MadFinn>: there's a catch—our moms
   wont let us go
<Bigwheels>: NO WAY bummer, my mom
   would
<MadFinn>: really?
<Bigwheels>: yours will too just get
   a good chaperone
```

Madison almost fell off her desk chair.
A chaperone?
Of course!

```
<MadFinn>: that's a great idea
<Bigwheels>: u can't go otherwise
   LOL
<MadFinn>: I know that '-)
<Bigwheels>: have u ever checked out
   the Nikki pages on the Web? They
   have a bulletin board on BFB, to
   look for the links there or do a
   search
<MadFinn>: <:>))
<Bigwheels>: GTG talk later bye
<Bigwheels>: *poof*
```

Madison swam around bigfishbowl.com for a

few minutes looking for other Nikki fans like the ones Bigwheels had mentioned. She didn't have to look for long before she found a fish tank (chat room) appropriately called NIKKI with 2,965 members. And more than 600 of them were online right now.

Most of the fans had written into the bulletin board pages with information about Nikki concert tour dates and locations, new Nikki photos posted on the Web, Nikki lyric sites, and other Nikki gossip. Many of the screen names revealed who were the bigger fans.

```
NIKKI4evah
iluvniki
sofineNikki
NikkiFan211
```

One of the postings was from someone near Far Hills who was desperate to get tickets to the upcoming local concert. Madison felt special knowing that they had tickets of their own.

And now, with the perfect chaperone, they'd be able to go—no problems from parents at all. But who would take them?

"Maddie?" Mom's voice jolted Madison out of her reverie so suddenly that she nearly knocked her mouse off the desk.

"Mom?" Madison said, logging off the Web and

turning around at the same time. "I didn't hear you come in."

"I don't feel much like cooking tonight," Mom said nonchalantly. "Do you mind if I order a pizza?"

When she was busy or distracted, Mom ordered out. Madison told her it was fine, as long as there were no weird vegetables on her slices. Mom had a tendency lately to order pizza with broccoli and spinach and other green stuff. She was a vegetarian, after all.

"You want root beer with that, right?" Mom asked, walking away.

Madison nodded absolutely. Root beer was her favorite drink. As it just so happened, it was Nikki's favorite drink, too.

She followed Mom downstairs to help clear off and set the table.

Brrrrring.

Madison reached for the phone, half expecting it to be Aimee or Fiona and half expecting it to be Dad.

But it wasn't.

Mrs. Waters was on the line. And she wanted to speak to Mom.

"Who is it?" Mom asked as Madison reluctantly handed her the telephone.

Madison shrugged. "Fiona's mom," she said softly.

Mom grabbed the receiver and gave Mrs. Waters

a giant "Hello." Madison sat down on a chair nearby and watched every facial expression on Mom's face. She was sure that her concert hopes could be dashed to pieces in the next few minutes.

And Madison didn't know what to do.

and need not enjoy to let any responsible Mom have
the way she that they or on hopes child of would be
To plan on the next lot and on.
and the place her there over...

Chapter 3

"We have to find the right chaperone, that's all,"
Madison told her friends at lunch the next day.

They were sitting together at their usual orange
table in the back of the lunchroom, ignoring their
guy friends Egg Diaz, Drew Maxwell, and Fiona's
brother Chet, who were seated at the opposite end
from them.

"My mom won't go for that," Fiona said. "Not
even a chaper—"

"No!" Madison interrupted. "My mom said that
your mom *will* go for it if we come up with a smart
plan about how we can go and who can take us. So
let's think. Who? WHO?"

Aimee picked at a leaf of lettuce on her tray and
sipped from a bottle of water. "I'm so bummed out."

"We should be celebrating!" Madison said.

24

"We'll be able to go. We have to think positive."

"Okay, okay," Fiona said. "My dad could drive us."

Aimee looked up and made a face. "I'm sorry, Fiona. No offense, but I'd be kind of embarrassed to go with your dad."

"Me, too," Madison admitted.

"Fine, then you guys name someone else," Fiona said.

"What about your dad, Maddie?" Aimee asked. "He's cool, right? Or his girlfriend Stephanie? She's pretty cool, too."

"Why is Maddie's dad cool and my dad isn't?" Fiona asked.

"My dad is cool in his own mind," Madison said, chuckling. She was remembering the many times he'd mortified her in public restaurants, at the bowling alley, and everywhere else they ever seemed to go lately.

Fiona giggled. "What about your dad, Aimee?"

"Are you JOKING?" Aimee laughed out loud.

"What about your mom?" Fiona asked.

Aimee paused. "Mom wouldn't go to a concert unless it was a folk singer or something. She's into all that music like Bob Dylan and the Beatles."

"Who's Bob Dylan?" Fiona asked.

Madison pounded her fist lightly on the table. "Come on, you guys! We have to think. We only have lunch period together today. That gives us twenty more minutes to come up with a perfect chaperone."

From the other end of the table, Chet leaned over to ask if he could eat his sister's dessert. She'd left half a brownie on her plate. As soon as he nudged over, Egg and Drew squeezed closer, too. Fiona blushed a little when Egg moved nearby. Her crush on him seemed to get worse every day.

"What's the deal—I hear you guys won tickets to some concert?" Egg asked the girls.

Aimee looked at him and smiled. "Yes, we did. Are you jealous?"

"Of tickets to a girly concert?" he said. "No, I don't think so."

Drew snorted. He did that when he laughed. "Nikki's cute," he said, half under his breath.

Chet put his hands up into the air and declared, "No, Nikki is superhot. There's a difference."

The girls looked at each other and smiled.

"So when is this concert?" Egg asked.

"In a week or so," Fiona said.

"And Mom is never letting you go, so give it up," Chet said.

Madison spoke up. "She will so let us go to the concert. We have it all planned."

"Yeah? What?" Chet asked. "You're bluffing."

"We are not. We're just not telling you guys," Madison said, practically shooing the boys away like bugs.

"Don't look now," Aimee whispered. "Her highness is coming over to this table, too."

Headed straight for the orange table was Ivy Daly, otherwise known in the Madison-Aimee-Fiona circle as "Poison Ivy." Ivy represented everything about seventh grade that Madison detested. She was a big show-off, and she tried to wield her Class President power around like some kind of weapon. Even worse, she liked the same exact boy that Madison did: Hart Jones. Fortunately, Hart was nowhere in sight right now.

"Hel-lo," Ivy whined as she stopped next to the table. Right behind her were her drones, two girls who followed Ivy's every move. Rose and Joan had also gotten their own bad nicknames over the years, too. Rose was Rose Thorn and Joan was Phony Joanie. The names fit them perfectly.

"Hello, Ivy," Fiona said. She spoke for the table. Madison and Aimee remained silent.

Madison noticed that Ivy was wearing a baby-T with the words "Sugar-Sweet" on it. She recognized that shirt as part of the newest Nikki fan-club package. Madison had wanted one of her very own, but the club had sold out of them by the time she requested hers. Madison's shirt was back-ordered for two months.

"What are you three doing this weekend?" Ivy asked.

"Who wants to know?" Aimee snapped back.

"I was just wondering," Ivy said. "Don't have a cow."

"Ivy has tickets to the hottest concert in town," Rose Thorn said.

Fiona looked confused. "Huh? *This* weekend?"

"No," Ivy said, smoothing out her T-shirt. "But this weekend I'm going shopping for the ultimate concert outfit."

"What concert are you talking about?" Aimee asked.

Poison Ivy and her drones laughed.

"Nikki," Phony Joanie blurted. "Duh. Who else?"

Fiona almost jumped in to say that they had concert tickets, too, but Madison quickly cut her off. She didn't want Ivy to know that they'd be there, too.

"Ivy, who's taking you to the concert?" Madison asked. She knew if Ivy had to admit in public that it was her mom or dad, she might get to see Ivy squirm a little. There was something so uncool about parental chaperones, as the girls knew. And Ivy wouldn't risk looking uncool around anyone—especially not at school.

"Actually, my sister Janet is taking me to the Nikki concert," Ivy explained. "You need to have someone who qualifies as an adult. I think they have to be sixteen or seventeen."

"Wow." Aimee had to admit it. "That's pretty sweet."

'Yeah, I guess," Ivy said.

"Are you two going to the concert, too?" Fiona asked Rose and Joan.

They just shook their heads.

"No, just me," Ivy boasted. "Tickets have been sold out since a half-hour after they went on sale. I'm one of the lucky ones. My dad knew some important people."

"Mmmmmm," Madison said. She glanced at Aimee and Fiona, who were doing their best not to laugh. "So where are you sitting at the concert?"

"In the fifth row," Ivy said. "I can practically reach up and touch Nikki right there on stage."

"Wow," Aimee said, faking a serious voice. "I'm soooo jealous."

Poison Ivy grinned. She thought Aimee meant it.

"Even better, I get to go backstage and meet Nikki after the concert," Ivy said. "My dad has a friend who—"

"How nice for you," Aimee said, cutting her off. She stood up with her tray still full of uneaten food and turned back toward the kitchen.

Madison and Fiona stood up, too, with their trays.

The bell for the end of the lunch period was about to ring.

"See you later," Fiona said as they walked away.

Ivy shrugged. "Yeah, later." She didn't like it much when people walked away while she was in the middle of speaking.

And Madison and her friends were good at that.

They hurried over to the dish area where they dumped their trays and leftover food.

"That was unbelievable!" Aimee said, trying hard to contain herself. "In the dictionary next to the word *fake* is a picture of Poison Ivy Daly—in that stupid T-shirt."

Madison chuckled. "Yeah."

"I thought us snagging tickets was special," Fiona said. "But I guess not."

"You guys!" Madison reminded them. "We still WON our tickets. We're in the FRONT row, not the fifth row. We *are* special. More than special."

"But we haven't decided on a chaperone yet," Fiona said. "Ivy has Janet. She's all set. What are we going to do?"

"If Ivy's bringing her sister Janet," Madison said, "it doesn't have to be a parent who goes with us."

"How about your brothers, Aim?" Fiona suggested. "They can drive."

"*My* brothers?" Aimee shook her head. "Are you kidding? They wouldn't be caught dead at a concert with me. All they do is pick on me for the music I listen to. Plus, they bother me."

"What about Roger?" Madison asked. "He won't pick on you."

Roger was Aimee's oldest and sweetest brother. He helped Mr. Gillespie run the front counter at Book Web, the family bookstore. He volunteered to feed senior citizens in the Far Hills neighborhoods with Meals on Wheels. Roger always did the right thing, said the right thing, and acted the right way, at least as far as Madison was concerned. He wouldn't be as embarrassing as a dad. He was twenty-three, the ideal chaperone age. And he was cute, too.

"Roger is too busy," Aimee said. "He's got a girlfriend now, and he's always with her when he's not at the store. He's a drag. You don't want him."

"He can't take us for one night?" Madison asked. "One dumb concert? Pleeeeeease."

"Yeah, Aim," Fiona joined in. "Pretty pleeeeeeease?"

"Well . . ." Aimee hedged. "I just don't—"

"You *have* to ask him," Fiona insisted. "Otherwise we can't go."

"Yeah," Madison said. "You wanna go, don't you?"

Aimee finally gave in. She said she would ask him that night. And she'd tell her mother about the concert, too. But she wasn't making any guarantees. In fact, she was certain he'd say no instantly.

Heee-ooooo! Heeee-oooo!

The girls jumped. Out of nowhere, a siren had started ringing. That meant fire drill.

"Okay, boys and girls," some teacher yelled from the faculty lunch table. "Order in the room! Fire drill!"

"Where's our Cafeteria Marshall?" another teacher asked aloud.

Madison, Aimee, and Fiona ducked out a side door and joined with the throng of kids parading down the main staircase into the school lobby. They had to file out in order and then meet up with their homeroom groups outside, across the street.

"See you guys later," Madison said, as she waved good-bye to Aimee and Fiona. They were in different homerooms. Madison looked for hers, for a sign that said A-F.

"Maddie!" a voice yelled out from the sidewalk. "Over here!"

Egg was standing with her homeroom group. Even though Madison often found him to be a pain in the neck, he was still one of her best friends ever. And he was definitely her best guy friend. Madison, Aimee, and Egg had all been pals throughout elementary school. Some old habits—and old friends—were hard to leave.

Madison clustered together with the rest of the kids from her homeroom, most of whom she usually never noticed. At today's fire drill she ended up standing next to a quiet girl she recognized from her science class.

"Aren't you in Mr. Danehy's section?" Madison asked the girl after a while.

"Yes," the girl said softly. She introduced herself as Carmen, but she didn't have much to say after that. She barely even smiled.

The longer Madison looked, she saw that Carmen

wasn't just pretty, she was prettier than pretty. Her long, thick, black hair rolled down her shoulders, and she had light, hazel-colored eyes. Carmen dressed really nicely too, like some magazine models. Her fingers and arms were long and thin and her skin was a pale brown color, as if she'd been to a tanning salon or something.

Carmen wore a plain sweater and spoke in a whisper, but none of that mattered to Madison. She stood there wishing that she looked and talked the same way as Carmen. She was suddenly self-conscious about her clothes, her hair, and even her feet. Madison quickly checked her own sweater for fear that she had food stuck on the front or cuffs. Carmen had on leather shoes with tiny buckles. Madison had on old sneakers.

"Line up in alphabetical order!" their homeroom teacher demanded.

It turned out that Carmen's last name was Forrest; and she ended up right behind Madison Finn for the duration of the fire drill. No one was supposed to talk, but Madison leaned in to talk anyway.

"Do you like Nikki?" Madison asked after a moment or two of silence.

Carmen shook her head. "Not really."

"Oh," Madison said. "How come? I think she's the coolest—"

"She's okay," Carmen said, cutting her off.

"Oh," Madison snapped back. She didn't

understand why Carmen had to be rude all of a sudden like that. Carmen was obviously like all the pretty girls. The prettiest girls in school always acted supersnobby.

Madison decided right there that Carmen was a supersnob.

"Okay," the teacher said. "We're going to file back into the school quietly, and you should all report directly to your next period class. Is that clear?"

Everyone pushed a little as they headed back into school. Madison's eyes scanned the crowd for signs of Aimee or Fiona.

Did they know Carmen?

Did they have any more ideas about the chaperone for the concert?

Where were they?

Up ahead, Madison saw a familiar, brown, curly head.

Hart Jones.

She hurried to catch up with him, but other kids kept getting in the way. Hart was probably headed up to art class, the same destination as Madison. She'd chosen art as a spring elective, and luckily Hart had ended up in the same section. They'd only met for class once before, so they hadn't picked final seats yet. Madison hoped that she'd be seated near her crush.

As they headed into the school lobby, Madison

nearly went flying. Egg caught her elbow. He'd been right behind her the whole time.

He was chattering on and on about some stupid new video game that he'd bought. He was obsessed with computers. Of course Madison loved them just as much, in a different way. But listening to Egg could get so boring—so fast.

Up ahead, Madison still had her eye on Hart, plowing through the crowd with his backpack on his back. But as he turned to head up the stairwell toward the art classroom on the fifth floor, Madison noticed something she hadn't seen before.

Hart was walking with another girl.

And that girl was Carmen.

Chapter 4

The art assignment in class was to draw a still life. Madison hung her head down in despair. She was floundering.

Mr. Duane, the art teacher, stood over Madison's desk, arms crossed, and looked at what she'd drawn so far.

"Is that a pear?" he asked, pointing to a green blob in the corner. "And is that a bowl?"

Madison shook her head. "That's supposed to be a hand."

"Oh," Mr. Duane said, patting her back lightly. "Well, keep trying."

They'd only been in class for ten minutes, and Madison already felt as if she were choking on old air. The greenhouse space where they took art classes was filled with warm, spring light, but it made Madison itchy all over.

Even worse, Hart was sitting across the room next to Carmen.

The students were organized into a semicircle. Everyone was drawing a still life of a bowl of fruit from a different perspective. Madison got stuck with the side that had a pile of pears. It seemed like everyone else was drawing way more interesting fruit, like bananas, apples, and grapes. Madison was sick of the green smudge on her paper.

She tore it off her desk pad and started another drawing.

Mr. Duane had made his way around the room by then to Carmen's desk. Madison watched as a smile spread across his face.

"Very fine," he complimented her, patting her back, too. "Lovely colors and use of the shapes."

Madison wanted to wipe the smile off Carmen's face, but she went back to drawing the fruit instead.

A few moments later, Mr. Duane excused himself. In addition to being the drawing, painting, and sculpting teacher, he was also the photography instructor. He had forgotten to turn off the faucets in the darkroom. He'd leave the art students for five minutes to draw.

"Why don't we turn on a little music for you," he said, turning on a beat-up-looking black radio and tape deck in the corner of the room. Classical music filled the air as he escaped into the dark room.

No sooner had he disappeared than some kids rushed the radio.

"Mr. Duane's music stinks," they said, and changed to a more popular radio station. Pop sounds filled the air.

I wanna be closer still
There's a place in my heart that you fill

Madison perked up. It was a Nikki song!

Luckily, everyone voted to turn up that station. Madison even started humming along. Everyone was.

I could be sugar-sweet like you
Sugar, sugar-sweet

The pears on Madison's paper actually seemed to look better as she sang along with the radio.

A few moments later, Egg's sister Mariah came into the art studio, and things got even better.

"What's up, Maddie?" Mariah asked, stopping next to Madison's stool.

"Hey," Madison said. She looked up at Mariah's cool orange hairdo. She was wearing all of her earrings in all of her pierces today, even though it was against the rules.

"Cool art," Mariah said, pointing to Madison's desk.

"Really?" Madison said with disbelief. "You don't think they look like trolls?"

"Oh," Mariah said. "What are they supposed to be?"

Madison sighed. "Pears."

"Oh," Mariah said again, recovering. "Yeah, I see it now. I was just looking at it from the wrong angle. Pears."

Mariah had come upstairs to drop off a few canvases from her freshman art project. She was one of the most talented artists at Far Hills Junior High, and Mr. Duane was helping her with a special spring exhibition of her work.

"What else is new?" Mariah asked.

"Well, we won tickets to a concert on the radio," Madison said. "A Nikki concert."

"For real?" Mariah said. "Who won? You and Aim and that new girl Fiona?"

"Yup. Only problem is that we need to find a chaperone now."

"Why not your mom?" Mariah suggested. "She's cool."

"I don't think we want to go with a mom," Madison said. "What about *you*?"

"I'm not old enough to be a chaperone, Maddie," Mariah said. "I mean, I would if I could, but—hey, you'll find someone else. I don't like that Nikki chick anyhow. She's so fake. Look, I gotta run."

Madison waved good-bye as Mariah walked into

the back part of the art studio. A cloud of gloom set-
tled back over her art desk.

The pears were still just smudges.

The Nikki song had stopped playing.

At lunch, Madison had been the number-one
cheerleader for Nikki and the concert, but now she
was feeling decidedly unoptimistic about the whole
plan.

Mr. Duane came back into the class and asked
everyone around the room to stand up and share.
This was the part of art elective that Madison, even
after only one class, had begun to dread.

The idea was to walk around the room in a circle
and examine everyone else's art. That way, you could
see how a group of people sitting in the same room
looking at the same objects could see something so
differently.

Madison walked to the desk next to hers and was
happy to see more messy pictures like hers. Not
everyone in the room was a natural artist; thankfully, she wasn't alone.

Around the room, some kids *had* drawn amazing
pictures, however.

Madison stopped to stare an extra-long time at
Carmen's art. She'd drawn a beautiful bowl of fruit
that actually looked like fruit.

Hart's picture was good, too. Madison hadn't
realized that in addition to being cute and funny, he
could draw, too. She felt one of those deep-down

pangs that only a crush delivers. Then she nervously saw that he was now standing directly across the room in front of her pears.

Gulp.

"Hey, Finnster!" Hart called out softly. He hadn't said hello before that, but now he was yelling across the classroom.

How embarrassing.

"What are these supposed to be?" he said, chuckling. Hart gave her a big thumbs-up. She wanted to melt into the floor. Was Carmen smiling?

"Now, class!" Mr. Duane announced as everyone arrived back at their original seats. "I have an assignment for you."

"Homework for *art*?" one kid cried. "Are you serious?"

"Of course," Mr. Duane said without batting an eyelash. "I'd like you to try drawing something else for the next class. In pencil."

"What?" the same kid yelled.

"Are you trying to get on my nerves?" Mr. Duane said.

The class laughed. The kid shut up.

"Now, as I was saying," Mr. Duane continued. "I'd like you all to draw a self-portrait for next week's class."

Madison's stomach flip-flopped. "Self-portrait?" she asked aloud, without even realizing it.

"You mean like in a mirror?" Hart asked next.

"Exactly," Mr. Duane said. "Examine yourself in a mirror, and then draw what you see. The important thing with this assignment is that you should draw the details like facts. Draw as if your face were a group of simple shapes, just as you did today with the apples and grapes. Try to toss away your ideas about what a face should look like. Follow the lines and curves you see in the mirror. . . ."

Mr. Duane's voice faded into white noise.

Madison wanted to run away. Her self-portrait would be nothing more than a page full of black-and-white blobs, just like the green blobs that were supposed to have been pears. Blobs were pretty much all she saw when she looked in the mirror lately, too.

Across the room, Hart and Carmen appeared to be whispering to each other. Was Carmen still smiling?

Supersnob.

Carmen's self-portrait would probably be picture-perfect, just like her.

Finally, the class bell rang. Madison grabbed her orange bag and tore out of the room. She headed downstairs toward the lockers, hoping to find Aimee and Fiona nearby. She could use some cheering up.

On the way down, she ducked into a girl's lavatory. As she was inside one of the stalls, she heard a bunch of eighth graders talking. One girl was applying lip gloss while the other two were gossiping.

Madison could see them through a crack in the door.

"I think I'm going to blow off that history test next week," the first girl said.

"You can't do that!" the second girl said. "You'll get detention."

"Like I care," the girl replied.

The third girl started describing an outfit she'd be wearing at the Nikki concert. The other girls oohed and cooed. Then they left.

The Nikki concert?!

Madison walked out into the main part of the bathroom by the sinks. She couldn't believe her ears.

Was absolutely everyone going to the concert— except her and her friends?

They had to convince someone to take them to the concert. And they still had to go and get *their* cool outfits for the show, too.

As she washed her hands, Madison looked into the mirror at her reflection. She couldn't believe that Mr. Duane had assigned a self-portrait for the next art class. Her picture would surely look like a troll— for real.

Madison leaned in closer to the mirror to wipe a spot off her forehead, but she was disappointed to discover that it was not removable.

In fact, this was no ordinary spot.

"Ahhh," Madison gasped to herself. "Zit."

Of course she had had pimples before, ones that could easily be masked with a slight dab of cover-up makeup and powder. But this was clearly no ordinary zit. This was a massive blemish-in-the-making. The more Madison looked at it, the redder it appeared.

In fact, it had mysteriously appeared during the school day.

The urge to run came over Madison again.

Run away, run away.

She couldn't believe she'd faced Carmen looking like this. Or Ivy. Or even worse—*Hart.*

They must have been laughing at her behind her back. It looked like a volcano brewing right there just above her nose. And it was only going to get worse.

Madison dug around in her orange bag for some powder or some kind of makeup to mask the blemish, but the only thing she could find was strawberry-kiwi lip gloss. That wouldn't do the trick. She wasn't about to give her super-zit a fine, gleaming shine. It was doing that well enough on its own.

Another girl came into the bathroom and went into a stall. Madison patted down her ponytails and rushed out.

Thankfully, it was the end of the day. And it was Friday.

She only had one thing left to do today, and that was to stop in and help at the animal clinic. Fiona had agreed to go with her, and they were going to take the bus across town together. Madison knew that the dozens of puppies and kittens waiting to be adopted wouldn't mind about the zit. That was some relief.

By the time she arrived at the lockers and met up with Fiona, Aimee had already left for her ballet class.

"She wants us to go to the dance studio to meet her," Fiona said. "Then she said we could go over to the bookstore and ask her brother about the concert chaperone thing."

Although they were far away from everyone's home and the neighborhoods of Blueberry Street and Ridge Road, the clinic and Aimee's dance studio were located only a block apart. This was a huge help with rides and car pools. Sometimes Madison's mom would drop them off and pick them up; other times, Aimee's dad would do it. His bookstore was just another short block away in downtown Far Hills, too. The three friends would coordinate their activities whenever they could, so hitching rides or hanging out together was easier.

As they shuffled out of the building, Madison saw Hart standing around with Egg. She didn't see Carmen; and that was a good thing, but she still didn't want Hart to see her.

"What are you doing?" Fiona said as Madison quickly tugged Fiona's arm in the opposite direction. "Wasn't that Egg over there? I wanted to say hi."

"Later, Fiona," Madison said, pushing through swinging doors into the school's main lobby. They went outside and crossed the street to take a bus together to the clinic. "We'll see them later."

"You're acting so weird," Fiona said, giggling. "What's going on?"

Madison collapsed onto the bench at the bus stop.

"I have a giant zit," she confessed, as if that explained everything.

Chapter 5

When Fiona and Madison arrived at the clinic, they were greeted by a rowdy Jack Russell terrier jumping around in the waiting area. He nipped at their heels and bags. Across the room, a terrified tabby cat hissed from the safe perch of its owner's lap. The owner hissed, too. There was a man to his left holding a giant iguana, also on a leash.

"Whoa," Fiona said. "It sure is busy around here."

"Wait until you see the main kennels," Madison said, taking Fiona through a set of doors into the back of the clinic.

Eileen Ginsburg, the all-around office manager and nurse, was seated at a computer terminal adjacent to the front desk. She had on one of her usual far-out T-shirts. Madison read the front: BEAUTIFUL IS A STATE OF MIND.

"Hiya!" Eileen chirped. "Who's your friend, Maddie?"

Fiona introduced herself. "I'm Fiona Waters, and I like animals very much," she said. "I always wanted a puppy."

"Is that so? Well, we got a whole back wall full of 'em. Have a look," Eileen said. "Oh, and by the way, Dan was looking for you earlier, Maddie."

Dan Ginsburg, Eileen's son and all-around volunteer at the clinic, also happened to be a Far Hills seventh-grade classmate of Madison's and Fiona's. He had been working with the clinic staff since elementary school, so he knew how to do almost everything there.

"Are you here for feeding?" Eileen asked.

Madison nodded. "And to show Fiona around. We'll be here about an hour, okay?"

"A few of the cages need cleaning, too," Eileen said, before disappearing back out front. "You don't mind taking care of it, do you?"

Madison gave her a funny little salute and then turned to face the back walls. All the dogs started to bark at once.

"Wow," Fiona said as they approached the kennel cages. "They're so loud."

"Yeah, you get used to it," Madison said. "Now, we just have to fill all the bowls with kibble. . . ."

"Is this the kibble?" Fiona asked, picking up a bag that read: 4-T-FY DOGGY MEAL. "I can't even lift it."

"Not from there," Madison said, showing Fiona the back bins where the dog food had already been opened and sorted. "You refill from here. Scoop it out and put it out. Easy."

They sorted and scooped for fifteen minutes.

"My hands smell like dog food now," Fiona complained. "Gross me."

"Mmmmmmmm," Madison teased in her best Homer Simpson voice. "Dawg food."

A little pug was nestled in a cage in the corner, whimpering. Madison couldn't take her eyes off him.

"It's mini-Phin!" she exclaimed. "He must be new here." She read his chart: GOOGLE. LIKES CARROTS.

Fiona giggled. "His name is Google?"

"People who volunteer at the clinic get to name all the pets when they come in," Madison explained.

All at once the radio on the overhead loudspeaker got louder, and everything suddenly stopped, including the dogs' barking.

"Do you hear that?" Madison asked.

Fiona giggled again. "I can't believe it."

Nikki was on the radio singing "Sugar-Sweet (Like You)."

And all the animals had suddenly gotten quieter than quiet.

Feeding and cleaning was much easier after that. Madison and Fiona fed the dogs and repapered most of the cages in only an hour. Work got done faster when the two of them were working together.

On the way out of the clinic, Fiona gave her mom a call to confirm if she'd be picking all three of them up at Aimee's dance studio. Mrs. Waters said she'd meet them there. Then Madison called home to tell *her* mom which parent was doing the chauffeuring from the studio; and when she'd be home later that evening. They waved good-bye to Eileen and the pets in the waiting room.

"See you two gorgeous gals around!" Eileen said as they walked away.

"Gorgeous?" Madison laughed.

Fiona laughed too. "Not as gorgeous as *moi*." She ran down the block toward the dance studio.

The neon sign outside Aimee's dance studio flashed MADAME ELAINE DANCE STUDIO in burnt orange. Aimee was on the fourth floor and the elevator was broken, so Madison and Fiona walked the flights up toward the classrooms. They'd never been there before now.

In the stairwell, they passed other ballet dancers with long, thin bodies. Madison noticed you could almost see everyone's ribs through their leotards. They were all so graceful, all arms and legs. The entryway into the dance studio was covered with taped-up flyers of the upcoming dance revue. Aimee's name was listed near the top of the flyer, which was impressive. She really was a superstar in this class. The rest of the notice board had pictures of famous dancers from American Ballet Theater. There was a photo of last year's class in costumes for *The Nutcracker*, too.

"You made it!" Aimee said, breathless, greeting her friends as soon as she saw them reach the top of the stairs at the fourth floor. "Come in, it's getting late! I want to introduce you to my teacher. Hurry!"

Aimee was one of the girls whose ribs were showing, too. Only for some reason she didn't look as graceful as the other dancers. She looked a little pale.

Madison and Fiona followed behind her, unsure of where to go.

"You guys!" Aimee nagged. She grabbed Madison's sleeve. "Come *on*!"

Madame Elaine was seated on a wooden chair at the corner of the room. A few other dancers were lined up around her and they were talking about pliés and pirouettes.

"Elaine," Aimee said, nudging one of the other girls to the side. "These are my friends. Is it okay if they watch?"

Madison shifted from one foot to the other. She felt so out of place in the studio, with her blue jeans and sweatshirt. Fiona twirled a braid in between her fingers and the beads clinked.

What were they doing here?

"Sit," Elaine instructed Madison and Fiona. She pointed a long, skinny finger toward a bench at the side of the room. Another mother and a little boy were seated there already.

"We're just doing a run-through," Aimee said. "You guys don't mind waiting awhile, do you?"

As Aimee walked away with her toes turned out to the sides, Fiona turned to Madison and whispered, "Do you think Madame Elaine is nice?"

Madison laughed. "She's mean looking."

"What's up with Aimee?" Fiona asked.

Madison shrugged. Something was distinctly different about her BFF's demeanor. Aimee wasn't really smiling. Her shoulders seemed to droop.

"Why is she in such a bad mood?" Fiona asked.

Madison shrugged again. "Maybe she has her period," she whispered, so no one could hear except Fiona.

"Oh," Fiona said. "I didn't think of that."

Neither Madison nor Fiona had gotten their periods yet. They'd talked about it a few times, but no one ever went into much detail. Who would want to go into detail about that? Every girl Madison knew was nervous that she'd get her period for the first time in the middle of gym class or right in front of some boy she really liked. Aimee had gotten hers the year before, but she never talked about it much. Madison wondered what things would shift once they all had their periods and they all got bigger chests. Would everything change when their bodies changed?

"Look at Aimee," Fiona said as the music started. "She looks so thin."

Madison nodded. She looked thinner than thin. You could actually see Aimee's hipbones in the leotard she was wearing. Usually, Aimee wore sweaters and layers, so neither Madison nor Fiona ever noticed her bones so much. Standing in the studio in her leotard and tights, Aimee looked too skinny, even for a ballerina.

"She looks sick," Madison said aloud, still looking at her BFF across the room. Aimee leaped into the air toward them, hands up in the air.

"Should we say something?" Fiona asked.

Madison shook her head. "She'll just get weird on us. She'll get all defensive. I think if she wants to look that way, she should."

"And she was so worried the other day about having one stupid cookie," Fiona remembered.

Madison sighed. Being superthin wasn't all it was cracked up to be. As the music stopped, Aimee wobbled over to her friends.

"I have to run through that one more time," Aimee said, losing her balance. She grabbed the barre.

"Are you okay?" Madison asked, reaching out for her.

"Of course," Aimee said, straightening up. "What are you so worried about?" Her voice snapped like a rubber band. Something was

53

definitely different. Madison didn't know what to say next.

"We'll wait for you here," Fiona said.

Aimee wiped her forehead. "Fine. Wait then. I'll be done in like a few minutes."

When the next run-through was complete, Aimee took Fiona and Madison into the changing room. She went into the bathroom stall to take off her leotard and tights while her BFFs waited outside.

"My stupid dance outfit is still too tight," Aimee said when she reappeared.

Madison and Fiona looked at each other with disbelief.

"Too tight?" Madison repeated.

Aimee threw her hands into the air. "Oh well, I'll fit into it eventually."

The three friends said a few good-byes to some of the other ballet students and then walked out of the studio. Mrs. Waters was there, waiting in her car by the curb.

"Hop in, girls," she said, giving Fiona a kiss hello.

Aimee and Madison crawled into the back seat together. Mrs. Waters headed toward the Book Web, Mr. Gillespie's bookstore. Despite all the distractions of puppies and dancing, they still had one clear mission this Friday afternoon: think of the perfect chaperone for the concert.

Of course, no one brought up the subject of the concert in the car.

Not with Mrs. Waters there.

The three friends were positive that Mrs. Waters would raise some loud objection, as she had been doing since they had won the tickets on the radio. She would start listing the reasons why they couldn't go, not ever, not under *any* circumstances. Fiona had warned Madison and Aimee that her mother was willing to talk about their attending the Nikki concert with an adult, but she was still uncomfortable with the whole idea of their being in such a huge arena with so many people. She was worried for her daughter's safety.

No one mentioned Nikki, the concert, or the tickets.

Fiona babbled about her soccer schedule instead.

As they drove on, Madison looked over and saw that Aimee had zoned out, staring through the car window. Usually Aimee was the chatterbox, but today she was the quiet one. And she looked very tired.

"Are you okay, Aim?" Madison asked.

"Huh?" Aimee said. "Yeah, I'm fine. Why?"

Madison didn't have a chance to ask anything else. They arrived at the bookstore a moment later.

Mr. Gillespie was decorating the front window as they walked inside. Behind him, Aimee's oldest brother, Roger, was working the register.

"Hey, girls," he called out when they walked inside. The door jingled.

Madison turned to Fiona. "I still think Roger should be our chaperone. I mean, he is way cooler than having one of our parents go, don't you think?

"Cooler than my mom, anyway," Fiona said. Her mom was still standing at the front entrance gabbing with Mr. Gillespie. "I still think she's going to figure out a way to stop us from going."

"No," Madison said. "My mom will make sure that doesn't happen. I promise."

"You guys," Aimee said, walking over toward her friends. "I have to help Roger with the cash-wrap area."

Madison knew that meant getting behind the front register. Aimee was good at wrapping books in the special Book Web wrapping paper.

"What about the concert?" Fiona asked. "We were supposed to talk about chaperones and figure out a plan."

Aimee shrugged. "Yeah, well I just can't right now."

"Are you okay, Aim?" Madison asked.

"Why do you keep asking me that?" Aimee replied. "I said I am *fine*. I'll call you guys later, okay?"

Fiona glanced over at Roger. "Maddie thinks Roger would make the best chaperone, Aim," she said.

Aimee groaned. "Okay, okay, I'll ask him. Will you guys please stop asking me?"

"Why don't we *all* just ask him," Madison suggested. "Right now."

The three BFFs looked at each other. Aimee groaned again, louder this time. "No, I said I would ask him," she said.

"I know, but—" Madison said.

"Fine!" Aimee said, thrusting her hip to the side. She was acting unusual. "I'll do it now."

They marched up to the counter and stood there, three across, staring at Roger Gillespie.

"What's up?" he asked. Madison thought she saw a twinkle in his eye. She really did have a teeny-tiny crush on him.

Aimee cocked her head. "This wasn't *my* idea," she said to her brother.

"What wasn't your idea?" Roger asked.

Fiona and Madison squeaked a little as they waited for Aimee to just spit out her question.

It felt like forever.

Chapter 6

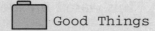

Good Things

Rude Awakening: Good things come to those who wait, especially when it's your BFF's older brother that you're waiting for.

Drumroll, please...

Roger said YES!!! He said it when Aimee asked him if HE would be our chaperone for the concert. And not only did he say yes, but he also said, "I'd be more than glad to go." MORE THAN GLAD! I thought Aimee was going to drop down right there on the floor she was sooooo surprised. He did say he might have a conflict or something with some meeting, but I know he'll come through for us!

Rude Awakening: Good things also come in

threes. (Gramma Helen always says that, and now I know it's true.)
1. Roger said yes.
2. Mrs. Waters changed her mind. Here's how that happened: After Aimee picked herself up off the floor, Fiona and I had to go home. We left Aimee there, and the whole way back to Fiona's house in the van, we talked about the concert and what we wanted to wear. Mrs. Waters was laughing at us. She actually said SHE was glad that we'd be going to the concert. What made her change her mind? ROGER!
3. We made a plan to go to the mall tomorrow on Saturday which is cooler than cool. That is the nicest surprise of all.

Madison closed the "Good Things" file. Before logging off her computer, she got a surprise, late-night Insta-Message.

<Wetwinz>: Maddie?
<MadFinn>: What r u doing up Fiona?
<Wetwinz>: I am so excited I can't sleep
<MadFinn>: NIKKI RULES We are gonna have soooo much fun @ the concert
<Wetwinz>: Did Aim call u tonite?
<MadFinn>: Nope, Y?
<Wetwinz>: She called me and she

```
        was acting wacky
<MadFinn>: ???
<Wetwinz>: said stuff about her
    dance recital again
<MadFinn>: like what?
<Wetwinz>: she thinks she's fat or
    something, I dunno
<MadFinn>: She is SO not fat what's
    up w/that?
<Wetwinz>: well n e way, I was just
    wondering
<MadFinn>: what time r we meeting
    tomorrow?
<Wetwinz>: Aim said ur Mom picks us
    up @ 10
<MadFinn>: ok well see ya
<Wetwinz>: WWBY
<MadFinn>: <:>))
<Wetwinz>: LOL
<MadFinn>: *poof*
```

No sooner had she bid good night to Fiona than Madison's laptop bleeped. She had new e-mail. Another surprise.

```
From: Bigwheels
To: MadFinn
Subject: Nikki
Date: Fri 17 May 8:21 PM
I just saw on TV that Nikki is
coming to Washington in a few
```

weeks. Isn't that cool? I think I'm going to try to win tickets on the radio just like you guys did. My little sister says she wants to go but I just laughed. Can you imagine bringing a little sister? What a drag!

Of course I already am thinking about who I'd have as a chaperone. My aunt Meg would be perfect—she dresses so hip. BTW: Did you find someone yet? Did you ask ur friend's brother like you said?

Yours till the pop stars,

Bigwheels a/k/a Victoria

With a smile across her face, Madison crawled under the covers with her pug, Phin, and scritched his fuzzy head. She was happy to know that she and her friends had found the right chaperone. Plus, this was the quiet time of day Madison liked best, right before sleep, when she could spend time all alone with her favorite dog in the whole world—and just think.

Madison's bedroom was almost blue with the glow from the moon. It was a full spring moon with a sky so clear that Madison could see different tree shadows dancing on her wallpaper. She'd cracked open the window just a smidge to let in some of the new air. There was a distinct smell in the air of lilacs that were just starting to bloom. The smell reminded Madison of her family the way it used to be. Dad had always clipped bunches of lilacs and put them in a bowl in the kitchen for Mom. Spring nights were also the time when Dad would come in to tuck Madison in—and softly sing doo-wop music in her ear.

Madison missed having Dad at home at times like this. But having Phinnie in bed made her feel safe.

"Rise and shine, honey bear," Mom bellowed, shaking Madison inside her blanket. "We have to go pick up your friends soon."

A groggy Madison wiped her eyes. "Huh?" she said.

Mom opened the curtains. Light poured in.

"Say hello to Saturday, Maddie," Mom said. "Upsy daisy."

Madison knew Mom had drunk about three cups of coffee already. She only acted this chipper after her daily dose of caffeine.

She rolled over.

"Hey!" Mom said, louder this time. She leaned in and planted a smooch on Madison's forehead. "We have a big day of preconcert shopping ahead of us. Get your tush out of bed!"

With that, Mom lifted the blanket clear off the bed. It was sunny in the room, but not too warm. Madison jumped up.

"Mom!" she said, rubbing her eyes some more. "Cut it out!"

Mom just laughed and disappeared out of the room. "Get dressed!" she said on her way out the door.

Madison threw on her jeans, a light cotton sweater, and her sneakers. She combed her hair back, because she didn't feel like washing it this morning. But there, in the mirror, she was horrified to discover that the blemish-in-the-making had gotten bigger. And redder.

"That is so gross," Madison said to her own reflection. She tried to comb her hair down instead of back, letting it flop in her face a little. That worked. The zit was hidden at least for now.

Whew. Maybe no one would notice.

After a quick breakfast, Madison and Mom drove the few doors down to pick up Aimee and then zipped around the block to Fiona's house.

"What's that on your forehead?" Aimee whispered to Madison in the car. "Did you get bit by a bug or something?"

"A zit," she said quietly. "An evil zit. Don't remind me."

Madison tilted her head so her hair would flop over the dreaded blemish even more.

"You guys, I can hardly think about homework or school or anything," Fiona said. "My mom contacted the radio station again this morning just to confirm that they'll have four tickets for us, and they said yes!"

Aimee made a face. "I guess it's cool. I just wish you hadn't made me ask Roger to come with us."

"Roger will be great," Fiona said. "Besides, who's going to pay attention to him at the concert anyhow? I'll be staring at Nikki the whole time."

"Yeah," Madison agreed.

Aimee crossed her arms and stared out the window. "It's a little embarrassing, if you ask me."

Fiona and Madison looked at each other, confused. Aimee didn't say much for the rest of the ride.

"We're heeeeere!" Mom announced as they pulled into the parking lot at the Far Hill Shoppes. "Who's ready to shop?"

Fiona and Madison laughed. "We are!"

Aimee forced a smile. "Me, too."

Usually, Aimee would have been the first person to hop out of the car and charge the mall. But today, she hung back. Madison grabbed one sleeve and Fiona grabbed the other.

"Let's go!" they said, pulling Aimee along. The three of them followed Madison's mom into the entryway at one of the larger clothing outlets.

"So girls," Mom said. "I imagine you three want to wander around and check out the stores. I have some errands to run. Why don't we meet back in an hour by the food court. We could grab some lunch there."

"I want tacos!" Fiona announced.

Madison smiled. "Sounds good, Mom. What if I want to buy something?"

"Well, Maddie," Mom said, "You have the money I gave you this morning, and if there's more I can go back to the store and look with you after we eat. How's that?"

During this exchange, Aimee wandered off a few yards to look in a shop window. It was a beauty salon with photos of hairdos and runway models. Aimee couldn't stop staring.

"What do you guys think of her?" Aimee said, calling her friends over. Fiona and Madison waved good-bye to Mom and joined Aimee at the window.

Aimee pointed to one of the models. "She doesn't look like a model, does she?"

"Why?" Madison asked.

"Well, she's too big to be a model," Aimee said. "And her hair is weird."

"Aimee," Fiona said gently. "Let's go look at clothes. Isn't that why we're here?"

Across from where they were standing, the girls noticed a huge display of CDs, posters, and video monitors along one wall at Spin Town, the record store where everyone shopped. A banner hung over the display.

NIKKI IN CONCERT! SUGAR-SWEETIE COMES TO FAR HILLS!!

Nikki's songs were being piped into the area outside the record store. Fiona read another poster on the store window.

WIN TICKETS! MEET WKBM INSIDE SATURDAY FROM 12 TO 3!

"You guys, look!" Fiona said. "We have to check it out."

The music got a little louder, as if someone had turned it up.

I could be sugar-sweet like you
Sugar, sugar-sweet

Madison laughed. A few girls around her were singing along. All of Far Hills was heating up with the news about the concert.

"And *we* already have tickets," Fiona bragged. "How lucky are we?"

"I think I'm getting sick of this song," Aimee said. "I mean, it's on every radio station every five minutes."

"But it's such a good song!" Madison said. "I'll never get sick of it."

"Me neither," Fiona added. "Come on, Aim, let's go in."

They followed a group of girls into the packed

store. Kids were lined up to win a chance for free Nikki tickets, courtesy of WKBM. In addition to free tickets, the radio station was giving out free CDs and posters, too.

"She looks so cool in that poster," Madison said as they passed by a display. Nikki was wearing a tight-fitting sweater-dress and little boots. Her hair was teased out, and she had on pink sunglasses.

"She is beautiful," Aimee said wistfully. "I really wish I looked more like her."

Madison noticed that when Aimee said that, Fiona walked away in the opposite direction.

"What's *her* problem?" Aimee asked aloud.

"Nothing," Madison said. "She's just going to look over there."

"Whatever," Aimee said. She walked in the exact opposite direction, leaving Madison by herself. Of course, Madison chased after Fiona. Aimee needed to cool off or something.

The three friends spent most of their shopping time inside the record store, watching Nikki on the monitors and listening to songs from her new CD. The store had listening stations where people could "sample" CDs before buying them. Madison and Fiona stood in one for at least fifteen minutes—until Aimee came back and tapped them on the shoulders.

"It's almost time to meet your mom," Aimee said. She was the only one who'd checked her watch. "Shouldn't we go to the clothing store now?"

Quickly, the trio pushed their way back out of the record store and into the bustle of the main causeway. Then they hurried over to Chez Moi, the girls' favorite casual boutique at the mall. They had so much to do and no time to do it.

In the window at Chez Moi, there was another gigantic Nikki display with posters and outfits set up on mannequins to mimic what Nikki was wearing in all of her photographs. They rushed inside.

On the left side of the store was an entire rack of cute T-shirts with even cuter designs. One had a miniature kitty-cat wearing a space suit. Another one said "Super Girly." A third had a tie-dye flower in the center. A sign on the rack said BUY TWO GET ONE FREE.

"Why don't we get T-shirts," Fiona suggested. "We can buy two and then the third one—"

"I can read the sign," Aimee said.

"Fine! But you don't have to be such a grouch," Fiona snapped back.

"I'm *not* a grouch," Aimee said.

"Hey, you two," Madison interrupted. "Why don't we look around some more before buying anything? The T-shirts will still be here in a few minutes if we leave and come back, right?"

They walked around the shop, examining every rack and table they saw. When Aimee picked out a tank top with blue sparkles, Madison and Fiona were thrilled with the thought that their BFF was finally getting into the shopping mood.

Until she tried on the sparkly top.

"My arms look flabby," she said, posing sideways in the mirror. "I can't wear this."

Madison frowned. "You have stick arms, Aim. It looks awesome."

"Yeah, seriously. Quit joking around and buy the top," Fiona agreed.

Aimee looked at her watch. "Maybe later. We have to go meet your mom now, Madison."

They made tracks over to the food court and found Madison's mom by the taco stand. Fiona was grinning as she ordered her taco with a side order of guacamole.

"I'll have a quesadilla," Madison said to the man behind the counter. "Cheese, please."

Mom ordered a bowl of super-hot chili.

"Aimee?" Mom asked last. "What do you want?"

Aimee shrugged and ordered a small taco salad, which ended up being a huge waste, since she only ate about three bites.

Across the food court, kids filed in and out with their parents or with their cliques of friends. Fiona got embarrassed when she looked up to see Egg and Drew standing way on the other side of the court. She got a case of instant shyness and refused to wave, walk over, or anything. Aimee got up and went over to say hello to the boys on her own.

Madison glanced around to see who else she could spot who went to Far Hills Junior High. As luck would have it, no cute boys seemed to be around, not even Hart Jones. Poison Ivy Daly wasn't around either.

But then Madison saw a familiar face, standing a little distance away.

It was Carmen, from science and art classes. She was at the mall with a bunch of other girls, some of them older like her mother and aunts.

She seemed picture-perfect, even from far away.

By the time Madison, Aimee, and Fiona left for home, the mall crowd was thinning out. Half the parking lot was cleared out, too. Madison knew some of this was due to the deadline at the WKBM booth. Everyone had departed after getting their free ticket chance and buying a signed CD or poster.

The girls carted huge bags of stuff back into Mom's car. Madison had gotten a T-shirt, and Fiona had gotten a glitter jewel belt for her jeans. Aimee had bought a pair of pink pants that were too baggy.

After dropping off Fiona and then Aimee, Mom asked Madison if Aimee was feeling okay. "She doesn't look well," Mom said. "She looks tired."

"Yeah," Madison replied. "She's been practicing dance like three times a day. She has a recital coming up next month."

"I think maybe I'll call her mother and see what's going on," Mom said.

They pulled the car into the driveway, and Mom went to take Phin for his late afternoon walk.

Madison went upstairs to her bedroom. Saturday evenings were usually busier than busy inside bigfishbowl.com, so she logged onto her computer to see who was online from her buddy list.

While waiting for the site to come up, she went into her files to write.

 Nikki

I have decided that Nikki is the best superstar despite what Aimee says. She always looks perfect in pictures, she has a great voice, she wears perfect clothes AND everyone loves her. What else is there left to be?

I wish I could be in her shoes for just one day. Sometimes I stand in front of the mirror in the bathroom and dream that I'm on some talk show being interviewed. The host wants to know all my secrets, and everyone is applauding very loudly. Nikki must have so many friends and boyfriends too. She's been on every awards show and every talk show in like 100 countries. What would it feel like to have everyone looking at you all the time? Meeting Nikki will be the most exciting time of my life so far.

Tomorrow I have to try working on that stupid self-portrait for art class. I wish I could look in the mirror and see someone

like Nikki looking back at me instead of my
plain old boring face—especially with
this weird zit that gets bigger every
day.
   I wonder if Nikki ever gets zits?
   Probably not.

Chapter 7

Sunday morning started with a thud.

Phin jumped up on Madison's bed and knocked her alarm clock off the nightstand.

"Rowrooooo!" he wailed, pug tail wagging. "Rowroooooooo!"

Madison bolted up in bed and headed for the bathroom, ignoring the clock pieces on the floor.

The zit was still there this morning, Madison noticed, grimacing. It was getting one of those little volcano tops to it, as if it would explode at any moment.

She wanted to pop it, but didn't. Having a hole in her face would be a far worse fate than having a volcano zit.

"At least no one has to see me today," Madison told her bathroom-mirror reflection.

That was some consolation.

If Sundays weren't reserved for baseball games or shopping, Madison would often spend them with Mom cleaning up around the house and doing other chores. Every since the Big D (divorce), the two of them had teamed up to keep the big house straightened up. Sometimes Mom would get a cleaning service in to steam the carpets and do the windows, but mostly she and Madison scrubbed and shined together. Now that spring was really here, there was a lot of cleaning to be done.

For housework, Madison wore her scrubbiest clothes: an old bandanna wrapped around her hair (which hadn't been washed now in two days), a goofy T-shirt with a rip in it, rainbow socks she'd had since fifth grade, and sweatpants that were two sizes too big and drooped down on her hips.

She was comfortable, that was what mattered. Or at least that's what she told herself.

"Hey, Mom," Madison asked as she went into the kitchen looking for some cereal and orange juice. "Can you tell I have a zit on my head?"

Mom peered up close into Madison's face. "You mean the one up there? Yes, it's a zit. But it's almost gone. And it's very small, actually."

"Quit lying to make me feel better," Madison

said. "It's twice as big as a pea, isn't it? It's huge. How can I go to the concert looking like this?"

"Maddie, stop," Mom said. "What are you worrying about *that* for? Aren't you supposed to be all excited today? The concert is coming up in only a few days, you have a new outfit—"

"I know! I am excited!" Madison blurted. "But this!"

"Just quit this obsession with the zit, honey bear. You're a beautiful girl. . . ."

Ding-dong.

"Okay," Madison said as she shuffled into the living room. "I'll quit obsessing. I'm a beautiful girl. See?"

Madison posed and pranced her way over to the front door. Smiling, she turned the lock without even thinking.

"Maddie?" the boy behind the door said as she flung it open.

Madison almost keeled over.

Hart Jones was standing there. Egg and Drew were right behind him.

She reached for the drawstring on her sweatpants and grabbed for the bandanna that was wrapped on her head.

"Hart?" she whispered. "Wha-wha-what are you doing here?"

Hart smiled wide. "Well, we just came by to see if you—"

"Nice outfit, Maddie!" Egg blurted. He burst into laughter.

Then Drew snorted.

Hart couldn't help but chuckle, too.

Madison felt her face, neck, and chest get hot. Her heart started to pound like a hammer. A drop of sweat traced its way down her back.

"I . . . um . . . look . . . I have to . . ." Madison stammered.

"Hey, Maddie, just chill out," Egg said.

"Yeah, Maddie," Drew said, echoing his friend.

"Look," Egg continued, pushing in front of Hart. "We're meeting Fiona and Chet over by the baseball field later for a game. Aim has dance practice, I guess. She didn't want to come. So we came by to get you."

"Baseball?" Madison said. "Today?"

"Yeah," Hart said, smiling. "Do you want to come with us?"

Madison's heart was still beating fast. She wanted to run, but her feet were glued to the hall floor.

"I can't play baseball—" she blurted.

"Why not?" Egg asked. "Just put on some sneakers and let's go."

Madison glanced down at her rainbow sock toes and her T-shirt, which just happened to have a splotch of breakfast cereal right on the front. She could feel her zit growing as she stood in the doorway. She could *feel* her dirty hair.

Help.

"I have to . . . have to help my mom with some work," Madison said, making up a quick excuse. "She's working on this really big film project and she needs my help. Sorry."

"Are you sure you can't come with us?" Hart asked. "I think it's going to be fun. Haven't seen you around much in school these days . . ." His voice trailed off.

"Nope, can't do it," Madison said. "Gotta run." She started to push the door shut, right in the boys' faces.

Egg pushed back. "If you change your mind, we'll be down at the far fields, okay? Maddie?"

"Yeah, sure," she said. "Okay. See ya."

"Bye!" Hart said, even after the door had been shut.

Madison peeped through the peephole. She should have looked through that first so she could have avoided the whole confrontation in the first place.

Egg, Drew, and Hart walked away slowly, tossing the baseball. Hart turned back once to look at the door. Madison wondered what he was thinking when he did that. Did he forget to say something? Was he still thinking about her ugly outfit? Was he deciding right there that he would never, ever speak to Madison Francesca Finn again?

Madison's entire body was covered in sweat by

now. She felt embarrassment wrapped around her like a winter coat that she wanted off . . . NOW! Madison ran into the downstairs bathroom and collapsed onto the side of the tub.

That's when the tears came. Floods of them.

"Maddie?" Mom said, knocking at the door a few moments later. "Honey bear, are you okay? Who was that? What happened?"

Sniffling, Madison got up and opened the bathroom door. Her kerchief was askew, her sweatpants were falling down, and her face was blotchier than blotchy from crying.

"Maddie!" Mom said, alarmed. "What on earth happened—" She ran cool water and dabbed Madison's face with a cloth.

"Hart . . . Egg . . . Baseball . . . Door . . ." Madison choked on the words.

"Honey!" Mom said in her softest voice. "Let's go sit down. What's going on?"

"Why is my life falling apart?" Madison asked her mom.

"Wait a minute," Mom said. "Last week we were all concerned about this Nikki concert. Now you're going, and you're sitting in the front row. That's like a dream come true. Why the tears?"

"Boys, Mom," Madison said. "I don't understand them. I'm not pretty enough."

"Where is all this coming from?" Mom asked.

Madison sniffled some more. "Aimee is acting so

strange, too. I don't know why, but things just don't feel right. Not even with front-row seats."

"I spoke with Aimee's Mom about her schedule—and not eating yesterday at the food court. She said that we shouldn't worry. Aimee's just nervous about performing. Aimee was never a big eater, anyway."

"Mom, it's more than that," Madison said, wiping her nose. "Ask Fiona. It's like Aimee isn't herself these days. I can't explain it. She has this weird faroff look. Didn't you see it?"

Mom thought for a moment. "Yes, I did. Maybe you should talk to her."

"I can't," Madison said. "She doesn't like talking. She gets all angry at me."

"That's not like Aimee," Mom said.

"Maybe it'll all go away when the concert comes," Madison said. "And we'll be three happy BFFs again. I just don't understand what's wrong. Maybe it was something I said or did?"

"I'm sure you're not responsible," Mom said, rubbing Madison's back. "You'll think of something to say. I know you will. You and Aimee have been friends for too long to let a few bad moods get in the way of your friendship."

"I guess," Madison said, readjusting her bandanna and blowing her nose.

"You know, I can give you some cover-up for that blemish," Mom said. "That way you won't have to worry about it when you have dinner with Dad tonight."

Madison grinned. "That would be great," she said.

"Hello, WKBM fans! Today we're playing all Nikki all the time! And now, let's hear her number-one hit single, 'Sugar-Sweet, Like You.'"

Madison turned up the volume on her clock radio, which she'd fixed after the morning incident. She sang along with Nikki, shouting as loudly as she could. "Sugar-sweet! Sugar-sweet."

She and Mom had spent the last few hours picking up the downstairs, gathering papers, dusting, vacuuming, and straightening closets. Now Madison was watering all the indoor plants while Mom cleaned the bathroom.

After the basic house chores were completed, Madison was happy to climb into the shower and wash her hair. She used all-natural lavender shampoo Mrs. Gillespie had given to Madison once for her birthday. Madison didn't use it that often, because she saved it for special occasions or times when she needed to feel special. Like now.

After showering, she pulled on a black dress from her closet. It had little yellow flowers on the fabric and was warm enough so she didn't have to wear a jacket. Madison wondered how she could possibly be feeling bad when spring was in the air. Spring was supposed to be like an injection of joy, with warm air and flowers and little bunnies hopping across the fields. So why did it feel like one big yuck?

She wrapped her hair in a towel and sat back down at her desk, booting up her laptop. This was one of those times when Madison had come to depend on one person above all others: her keypal.

Madison opened her e-mailbox and hit NEW.

```
From: MadFinn
To: Bigwheels
Subject: HELP!!!
Date: Sun 19 May 2:11 PM
```
I miss you! My life is falling apart. What am I supposed to do? Where r u?

I have a zit the size of a walnut on my head and it shows no signs of letting up.

My BFF Aimee is an alien. Well, not really, but she's acting weird these days. Everyone thinks so. I'm really worried about her. I think maybe she has anorexia or something. We talked about that last year in health class. I know that is like superserious, but it's true—she never eats food anymore and she looks too skinny. It's so weird to think anyone could be TOO skinny, but she is. She was never like this before. I don't understand what happened.

Did I also mention that I am probably never going to go on a real date with Hart either, since he saw me today looking soooo ugly. I'll be surprised if he ever talks to me again. Plus, I think he likes this OTHER girl better than me, and she is in my art class and she is a supersnob so I don't have a chance. Girls like her always get their way.

The only good thing—and it is a VERY VERY good thing—of course, is the Nikki concert. I think my whole life is gearing up for that one moment. Is that dumb? I have no idea what to wear, but whatever. I'll figure it out at the last minute like I always do.

Do you have any advice for me? You are so good at figuring stuff out. What's new in ur world?

Yours till the life lines,

MadFinn

After hitting SEND, Madison noticed that there was an e-mail already waiting inside her mailbox, too. It was from Dad. She panicked for a split second, fearing that Dad might cancel. He did that sometimes.

But he was just checking in. He'd sent his e-mail to her that morning.

```
From: JeffFinn
To: MadFinn
Subject: Dinner
Date: Sun 19 May 9:31 AM
Dinner is still on for tonight. I
think we're going to add a little
surprise too—a baseball game, with
Stephanie. It's a local league
playing in the next town over. I
got us tickets for this night game.
We can hang out and have fun. Wear
your jeans, hon. I'll be over to
pick you up around five o'clock.

Love, Dad
```

Madison sighed. She stood up, walked into the bathroom off the hall, and stared into the mirror.

"I can't believe I have to change again," Madison said to her own reflection. "I'm so sick of changing."

She pulled off the black dress and grabbed a pair of faded jeans.

Then she applied a little more of Mom's zit cover-up just to be safe.

Dad would be over at any moment.

Chapter 8

In the car on the way to the baseball game, Dad and Stephanie listened eagerly while Madison recounted the entire concert ticket-winning experience.

"Sounds like you've been having a busy week," Dad joked.

"And this is your first concert?" Stephanie asked.

Madison nodded and leaned into the front seat a bit so she didn't have to yell when she spoke. "Actually, it's the first concert for all of us."

"How exciting," Stephanie said. "I remember my first concert, don't you, Jeff?"

"Oh yeah, I went to see the Rolling Stones," Dad said. "Those were fun times."

"I can't imagine you at a concert, Dad," Madison said.

"I was probably sixteen or so when I went to see the Allman Brothers," Stephanie remembered.

"Does your mother approve of this whole concert thing?" Dad asked. He sounded a little concerned. "You are being chaperoned?"

Madison reassured him. "DAD!" she said. "Of course! We have it all planned. Aimee's brother Roger is taking us."

"Is he responsible enough?" Dad asked.

"Jeff, will you just let her enjoy this? Stop worrying!" Stephanie said.

She turned around to face the backseat and grinned.

"Next time you're looking for a chaperone, Maddie, you should call me!" Stephanie said. "I love Nikki's music."

Madison grinned back. "Yeah, that would have been cool. I'll remember that for next time."

They pulled up to the West Lake ballpark just as everyone else did. Guys in baseball caps were out directing the traffic.

Madison hadn't known what to expect, but the "stadium" consisted of nothing more than a regular baseball field with bleachers on two sides. Huge lights on towers cast a glow around the field and parking lots. A funny-looking man working a frankfurter-shaped food cart by the entrance to the field cried out, "Soda! DOGS!"

"It's open seating," Dad said. "Let's go over to

that side where there aren't as many people. On the third-base side."

"Do you want anything to eat, Maddie?" Stephanie asked. "We're going to dinner afterward, but if you want something now, we can—"

"Nah," Madison said. "I don't eat dogs."

The crowd transfixed Madison. This place was packed! A few men with giant bellies sat down in the bleacher seats just ahead of them, laughing in that really annoying, loud way that strangers do.

Other people filed in and sat down on the surrounding bleachers. It was overwhelming to notice all the different faces and clothes and body types. For some reason, Madison had her people radar on tonight. She was observing and taking mental notes on all kinds of people: fat, skinny, tall, short, and loud.

There were definitely lots of *loud* people here. The men in front wouldn't shut up. But the weather was warm and balmy. Spring was definitely here, and everyone, loud or quiet, seemed happy.

Each league team was sponsored by a local business. A family of eight came into the game wearing blue and yellow, the team colors for Winnie's Dry Cleaning Astros. The opposing team wore red and white and called themselves Freeze Palace Pirates. Madison smiled when she saw their name, since she and her friends always got their ice cream at Freeze Palace. Now she knew what team she'd be rooting for.

When Dad got up for some popcorn, Stephanie leaned over to whisper to Madison. "I meant to say earlier that you look adorable tonight," Stephanie said. "I love that sweater. And did you change your hair?"

Madison's hair was still flopping in her face. As of this week, she thought of it as her new, zit 'do.

"Well, sorta," Madison said. She hedged, but then decided to come clean with Stephanie. Lifting her bangs, Madison revealed the giant, hidden pimple.

"What's so bad about that?" Stephanie asked. "You can barely see it."

"Thanks for lying," Madison said. "But I know a volcano when I see one. It ruins my entire face—and if it weren't for the cover-up that my mom gave to me . . . and I have to go to the concert looking like this!"

"Maddie," Stephanie said. "You are so lovely, don't you see that?"

Madison felt uncomfortable when anyone started giving her these little pep talks, but she listened anyway.

"When I was in seventh grade," Stephanie went on. "I once had this huge rash break out all over my face. I thought it was hives or an allergy or something. Then the doctor told me it was acne. Acne!"

"Bummer," Madison said, listening a little closer now.

"Well, I freaked out. Acne was like being a leper, at least at my school. I stayed home for three days until my mother finally told me I had to go back. Even then, I'd sit in class with my head down, eyes on the floor. I didn't want anyone to see me, least of all the guy I liked in my homeroom, Bobby MacPhee. The kids laughed at me and called me crater face and all sorts of mean stuff. It was awful."

Stephanie kept talking about her junior-high experience. How *her* invasion of pimples had lasted for months. How she'd tried every medicine that was available.

"How did you ever get through it?" Madison asked.

Stephanie shrugged. "Took zit pills and smeared on cream and lots of cover-up. But more importantly, I learned something."

"Learned something from zits?" Madison said.

"Yeah. I learned who my real friends were. They didn't care about any of the cover-ups. They loved me whether I had zits or not. I think I was afraid they wouldn't. Isn't that silly?"

Madison wondered if Hart liked her just the same, now that he'd seen her great zit.

"The point is, Maddie," Stephanie explained, "sometimes I think we look into the mirror and focus all our attention on one thing, one flaw. But most people looking at you from the outside don't see that flaw. They see the whole you. They see the cute face, the fun hairdo, the seventh-grade computer whiz. Got it?"

Madison nodded, even though she wasn't sure she did.

"Maybe," Stephanie said, laughing, "you should stop looking in the mirror for a few days. No one's perfect, Maddie."

"I know," Madison said with a sigh. "I know."

"Hey!" Dad yelled, reappearing just a few rows down. He was walking back up the bleachers with his popcorn and a few drinks. "They're about to take the field."

Madison glanced around the ballpark again, looking for signs of someone—*anyone*—she knew. But everyone started to blend together in a sea of baseball caps, hot dogs, and chatter.

"PLAY BALL!" the umpire yelled from down on the field.

A cheer went up from the stands.

Madison cheered, too.

"Hello? Mom?"

When Madison came back home after the game and a quick dinner at Dad's favorite Chinese restaurant, she looked for Mom right away. Poking her head into Mom's office, she found her slouched in a chair, half asleep.

"Mom?" Madison whispered, gently shaking her mom's shoulders. She'd been working late on a project.

"Oooh!" Mom jumped up, awake in an instant. "I must have dozed off. What time is it?"

"After nine-thirty," Madison said. "Dad just dropped me off."

"Did you have fun?" Mom asked, half yawning.

Madison nodded. "You and Dad used to watch baseball all the time together, didn't you? I thought of that when we were there."

"Oh, Maddie," Mom said, leaning forward to give her daughter a warm hug. "That was sweet."

"I like Stephanie so much, but sometimes I still miss you and Dad being together. Is that weird?" Madison asked.

Mom shook her head. "Not one bit. Hey, let's get ready for bed, okay? We can talk upstairs."

When Madison climbed up, she was surprised to discover that Mom had laid out a spread of beauty moisturizers and buffers and all kinds of special products on the bathroom counter.

"I thought maybe I'd give you a mini-facial before you went to sleep," Mom said, smiling. "Not a real facial, but a little pampering. We can all use that."

Madison glanced in the mirror and saw the zit staring back at her. She remembered what Stephanie had said about forgetting and letting go. Mom believed the same thing. Maybe Madison could, too?

She and Mom perched on the edge of the tub. A half-hour later, after lots of lotion and good laughs, Mom pronounced Madison "beautified."

Madison had to admit that she felt nicer than nice.

Her zit even felt invisible.

After saying their good-nights, Madison pulled on her oversized Lisa Simpson T-shirt and turned on her laptop. She hadn't spoken with Fiona or Aimee all day, so she surfed through the chat rooms on bigfishbowl.com and checked her buddy lists in search of a little conversation with her BFFs.

No one she knew was online right now, so she checked her e-mail next.

FROM	SUBJECT
✉ Webmaster@bigfis	Site Updates
✉ Bigwheels	Re: HELP!!!

The Webmaster at bigfishbowl.com sent a general announcement to all members about the site. They were adding new features to the "Ask the Blowfish" fortune-telling page; developing new and improved chat rooms; and working on the creation of a MAKE YOUR OWN WEB PAGE section. Madison wanted to pay extra-close attention to that part. She was always looking for new ideas to improve her own Web use and the Web pages on the Far Hills Junior High site.

However, the second e-mail was way more important. Madison really wanted to hear from her key-pal. Bigwheels had sent it just a moment before.

From: Bigwheels
To: MadFinn
Subject: Re: HELP!!!
Date: Sun 19 May 9:31 PM

I miss you too and I'm supersorry that I have been bad about writing back. I have too much homework these days. And it is soooo funny that you said you have a zit, because I get those too and they are AWFUL. But it will go away eventually. My mom took me to a dermatologist once and she gave me this cream for it.

I wouldn't stress out about your BFF. Aren't all dancers supposed to be really skinny? If you are really worried though, just tell her. And as far as your total crush goes, maybe this Hart guy isn't the guy for you. I mean, why do you like him so much anyhow? That other girl sounds mean. She probably knows you like him and is doing it on purpose! I agree that girls like her always get their way. That's how I feel sometimes at my school too.

I am wicked jealous of you going to the Nikki concert. My mom says that

maybe if Nikki comes here to play
(I think she has a concert in
Seattle), then I can go—MAYBE. But
I have to do all these chores and
pay for part of the ticket. I want
ALL the details from when you go
like who you see and meet and what
songs she plays and EVERYTHING!!!

BTW: Have you checked on a search
engine lately for Nikki Web pages?
I checked, and found that there
were 133,489, and that Nikki is the
most popular search term. Can you
imagine having that many different
Web pages with your picture on
them? I have to go download some
pictures and print them out. One
entire wall in my bedroom is
devoted to Nikki. My fave poster
is this shot of her from the latest
issue of Teen Blast. She has on
this very cool dress and pink
glasses.

Write back soon and tell me what
happens with everything.

Yours till the super stars,

Bigwheels (a/k/a Victoria)

94

Just as Madison hit SAVE, another message popped into her e-mailbox.

Madison caught her breath when she read the name.

FROM   SUBJECT
✉ Sk8ingBoy   Class

She stared at the screen, dumbfounded. Sk8ingBoy was Hart Jones!

Hart had first asked for Madison's e-mail address months ago. So what made him send her e-mail *today*? Madison opened it up quickly.

From: Sk8ingBoy
To: MadFinn
Subject: Class
Date: Sun 19 May 9:40 PM
Hey Finnster have u done that
self-portrait for art class yet? I
dont know whattodo for mine. Do we
ned it for class 2morrow? I am
gonna call Carmen about it. Write
back soon. CYA L8R.

Madison could hardly catch her breath. Her crush had finally sent e-mail.

But Madison sighed.

Hart was going to call Carmen?

Between enemy number one, Poison Ivy Daly, and supersnob Carmen, competition for Hart's attention in seventh grade had gotten so fierce. With (or even without) the great zit, Madison was beginning to realize that maybe Hart would never think of her the way she wished he would. He'd never crush back.

She quickly tried to get her mind on other things—like Nikki.

Madison's first concert was now only a few days away.

Chapter 9

At the lockers Monday morning, Fiona and Madison were standing around gabbing about the upcoming Nikki concert, when Aimee walked up. She had a sour expression on her face.

"Aim!" Fiona said. "So how was the rest of your weekend? Did you find an outfit for the concert?"

"I guess," Aimee said, opening her locker without saying another word. She just gathered her books, shoved them into her bag, and walked away toward class.

"Aim?" Madison called out after her. "Wait!"

She and Fiona chased after their BFF.

"Are you feeling okay?" Fiona asked. "You didn't answer my question."

Aimee shrugged. "Yeah. I'm okay. Why do you keep asking me that?"

"Because," Madison said, "you seem kind of distant."

"You guys are acting so weird lately," Aimee said.

"*We've* been acting weird?" Madison said. "Are you joking?"

"No," Aimee replied. "You keep asking if I'm okay. Why don't you just leave me alone? I am fine. I am excited about the concert and I am fine."

"Aim!" Fiona said, smiling. "Come on. We're just—"

"Just *what*?" Aimee interrupted.

"Aim, what is up with you?" Madison asked.

"Yeah," Fiona said. "You never talk to us like—"

"Like *what*?" Aimee asked. "You guys, I'm psyched about the concert and all that—okay? But I have other stuff on my mind, too. So would you please stop asking me the same questions? Just leave me alone."

Madison and Fiona just stood there with nothing to say.

Brrrring.

"That's the bell. I have to go to class," Aimee said. "Are you coming, Fiona?"

Fiona grabbed her stuff, too, and gave Madison a look as she walked off.

It was as if someone had stolen the real Aimee and replaced her with a ballerina clone.

Madison said a quiet good-bye and watched Aimee and Fiona as they disappeared around a corner. Then she grabbed her books and headed off to her English class. There was a busy morning of quizzes and essays ahead, and she was planning to spend the afternoon in the computer lab helping Mrs. Wing, her favorite teacher, with updates to the school's Web site.

Later that day, when Madison arrived at the computer lab, Mrs. Wing was busier than busy. Other kids were milling around, too, including Egg and Drew. They were scanning in photos for the site.

"Nice of you to show up," Egg cracked. "What are *you* doing here, Maddie?"

She hadn't been by the lab to help after school very much this spring. Madison's volunteering and schoolwork had been taking up most of her time.

"Hiya, Maddie," Drew said sheepishly. Madison was beginning to think maybe Drew liked her from the way he acted around her, all shy and sweet. But there was no way she wanted to think about that, so she just smiled.

"Don't act so surprised that I'm here, Egg," Madison said. "I've been busy, that's all."

Egg made a face. "Yeah, right."

Madison gave him a knuckle noogie on his shoulder, and Egg let out a little "Ouch."

"We were just downloading pictures from the last soccer games," Drew said.

"There's a really good shot of Fiona, actually," Egg said. "Wanna see?"

Madison grinned. "How *is* Fiona, Egg?" she asked.

Egg turned beet red. "How should I know? Duh. You see her more than me."

Madison grinned even wider. "Yeah, right."

As Egg and Drew continued scanning, Madison placed the photos in a collage on the soccer page. She wrote some captions, too.

GOALIE JUST MISSES THE BALL!

FAR HILLS FORWARD DAISY ESPINOZA ON THE GO!

GAME-WINNING KICK FOR THE RANGERS!

They had only been sitting there working for a short time when someone barged right into the classroom. Egg's mouse almost slid off the desk.

It was Fiona.

"Oh, Maddie, you're here!" Fiona said, breathless, running over to the terminal where Madison was seated. "You won't believe what just happened. I was in last period standing next to Aimee and she . . . she . . . collapsed."

Madison shook her head. "What?"

"Like, onto the floor?" Drew asked.

Fiona caught her breath. "She was standing there normal one minute and then the next minute she was lying there in a heap. Roger and her dad came over like ten minutes ago from the bookstore to pick her up. Nurse Shim was freaking out. It was so awful."

"Where is she now?" Madison said.

"Home, I guess," Fiona said. "Yeah, that's what Nurse Shim said."

"I hope she's not really sick," Egg said. He sounded worried for real.

"Let's go!" Madison declared. She grabbed her orange bag and asked Egg and Drew to take over the rest of the computer scanning.

"Go where?" Fiona asked.

"Over to Aimee's, to see if she's okay," Madison said.

The walk back toward the Gillespie house on Blueberry Street felt like an eternity. Bags felt heavier, sidewalks seemed longer, and the air even seemed hotter.

"I bet I know what happened," Fiona said as they trudged along. "She wasn't eating. That can make you faint, right? Like the other day at the mall, she made fun of our lunches. She's *always* talking about not eating."

"I guess you're right," Madison sighed.

"I know you guys have been friends way longer than I have been," Fiona said. "But not eating and getting so angry in class . . . I've read magazine articles . . . this kind of behavior can be wicked serious."

"You sound like a doctor or something," Madison said.

"It's true, Maddie!" Fiona said. "Didn't you read *The Best Little Girl in the World?* Haven't you seen those TV movies? I think Aimee is anorexic."

Madison sighed. She knew what Fiona was saying. This didn't seem real. How could it be happening to their friend?

They pushed themselves to walk a little faster. Thankfully, the Gillespie house was in view. Aimee's brother Roger had just walked out onto the front porch.

"Roger!" Madison cried out. "Is Aimee home?"

Roger had his head hung down low. "Did you guys see what happened to my sister?" he asked.

"Aimee fainted," Fiona said.

Madison nodded. "Fiona was there."

"The doctor is up there with her now," Roger said. "He said her blood sugar was low. Apparently, she's dehydrated, too. He says she may have been starving herself."

Madison and Fiona grabbed each other. "Is she going to be okay?" they asked at the exact same time.

"The doc says she's lucky nothing worse happened. But—" Roger cleared his throat. "You guys are with her all the time. Did she stop eating or what? I want to know why she did this to herself. What did she say?"

Just behind them on the street, Mrs. Gillespie pulled up in her car and drove into the driveway. She rushed past them, asking Roger if Aimee was upstairs. She was holding her cell phone. Madison was sure that Mr. Gillespie had called her right away.

When Mrs. Gillespie said that it was all right to see Aimee, Fiona and Madison went upstairs. Aimee looked paler than pale. Her skin was as washed out as her bedsheets. But she still managed to say hello.

"Wow, everyone's here," Aimee said.

The doctor was retaking her blood pressure. "Keep still," he cautioned. "You need to stay very quiet. Close your eyes, Aimee."

Aimee's eyes were droopy. She looked over at her friends. "I messed up. I'm sorry."

"You rest, Aimee," the doctor said. Then he told everyone to step outside so Aimee could sleep.

"Just as I suspected, your daughter passed out due to lack of nutrients and insufficient hydration," the doctor said. "Have you noticed any changes in her behavior lately? Has she been more irritable?"

Mrs. Gillespie shook her head. "She has been dancing a lot. Probably too much, I guess," she said. "Have you noticed anything strange, dear?" she asked her husband.

He shook his head and asked Roger the same question.

"I barely see her, Ma," Roger said. "She dances nonstop, every day. She's obsessed with it."

The doctor listened closely, nodding. "Anything else?"

The Gillespies shook their heads no.

"Actually," Madison spoke up, "we've noticed

some changes in Aimee." She glanced over at Fiona.

"We have," Fiona agreed. "Aim seemed upset lately."

"Upset?" Mrs. Gillespie said. "About what?"

"Dance mostly," Madison said. "She didn't fit into her costume or something. And she was talking about the way she looked a lot."

Mr. and Mrs. Gillespie hugged each other.

Roger shook his head. "Does she have an eating disorder?"

The doctor frowned. "Sounds likely that she was on the way to that, but I don't think it was anything quite that serious—yet."

He escorted the Gillespies down the stairs and into the kitchen, where they sat around the table talking about what to do next and how to get Aimee healthy again. Madison and Fiona asked to say a quick good-bye to Aimee. She hadn't fallen asleep yet.

"Thanks for coming, you guys," Aimee said when her BFFs appeared in the doorway.

"We were soooo worried," Fiona said.

Madison sat on the edge of the bed. "Why did you stop eating, Aim?"

Aimee moaned. "I felt fat. Everyone in dance is better than me."

"Aimee!" Madison said. "You're so skinny. What are you talking about?"

Aimee started to cry. "I'm so sorry," she said.

"Why are *you* sorry?" Fiona asked. She sat on the other edge of the bed. "You're the one who's sick."

"I messed everything up," Aimee cried. "Now I'm sure Dad won't let me go to the concert, either. I ruined everything."

Madison and Fiona looked at each other across the bed. No concert would be bad news. They hadn't thought about that consequence. But they didn't want Aimee to feel badly about it.

"Don't worry about the concert right now," Madison said. "It's not until the end of the week. Maybe you can still go."

Aimee sniffled. "I doubt it. When my dad makes up his mind to something he usually never changes it. And Roger *always* sticks with Dad. So he probably won't be going either as the chaperone. We're doomed."

"Quit worrying," Fiona said as she stroked Aimee's forehead. "You have to get better first."

"Yeah," Madison chimed in. "You *will* get better. We're not doomed. Not yet."

Aimee was still crying a little. "I was so mean to you guys in school today. I'm sorry for that, too. I wouldn't blame you if you never talked to me again."

"Aimee!" Madison exclaimed. "Will you stop talking like this?"

"We're your BFFs," Fiona said.

"We love you," Madison added.

"You guys are such good friends," Aimee said. "I love you, too."

The three held hands on top of the blankets, squeezing extra tight.

After a few more minutes, Madison and Fiona left for home. Their mothers would be wondering why they hadn't returned home from school yet. And they both had bags filled with homework.

It had been a wild week already—and it was only Monday?

The Nikki concert was four short days away.

Chapter 10

From: MadFinn
To: Bigwheels
Subject: You Won't Believe This!!!
Date: Tues 21 May 4:23 PM
___

Wow do I have a story for you.
Well, remember how I said my BFF
Aimee was acting all weird? She
passed out in school yesterday!!!
Thankfully she's OK though. Her mom
says she'll be OK to come back to
school in a few days. She just
needed to rest and EAT. She was
obsessing sooo much about her body
lately she stopped eating!!
Personally, I couldn't IMAGINE not
eating.

She's a ballet dancer, I told you that, right? I think Aimee wished she could be the skinniest one in her dance class. Aimee's ballet teacher actually went over to her house and talked about what happened. Aimee said everyone was telling her she can't starve herself if she wants to be a dancer because she can't dance well if she is weak. The idea of NOT dancing freaked Aim out so much that she agreed to go on this special diet supervised by her mom (who is this health nut) and her dance teacher (who is this superstrict crazy lady). Aimee has to write down all her meals and bring some high-protein lunch to school and take vitamins. Sounds gross to me, but she'll do N E THING to dance.

I don't think I ever asked, R U a dancer? I am most definitely NOT one. My friend Egg told me once I had the opposite of rhythm, whatever that is.

I'm of course glad she's OK but NOW we have to figure out a way to convince Aimee's parents that she

should be allowed to go to the
Nikki concert. It's 3 days away.
I'm afraid after all this happened,
they won't let her go ANYWHERE.
What do u think??? WBS.

Yours till the spring rolls,

MadFinn

Madison hit SEND and waited for the message that
said her mail had gone through. Then her computer
beeped.
She had an Insta-Message.

<BalletGrl>: MADDIE, HELP!
<MadFinn>: What r u doing online
    shouldn't u b in bed or some-
    thing?
<BalletGrl>: The worst thing ever
    has happened
<MadFinn>: Worse than u getting sick
<BalletGrl>: OH MYGOD sooooo much
    worse!
<MadFinn>: :-6
<BalletGrl>: Roger wont go
<MadFinn>: huh? where
<BalletGrl>: To the concert! He sez
    he CAN'T
<MadFinn>: Because of what happened
    in school?

\<BalletGrl\>: No, that's not it. Mom
    says no prob we can still go 2
    the concert except not w/o a
    chaperone
\<MadFinn\>: What did Roger say?
\<BalletGrl\>: He's busy. DUMBO
    EXCUSE. I think he has some work
    or a date I dunno I HATE HIM
    RIGHT NOW
\<MadFinn\>: Oh no
\<BalletGrl\>: Oh my god what r we
    gonna do?
\<MadFinn\>: We'll think of something.
    I can ask Stephanie my dad's gf
\<BalletGrl\>: THAT'S GREAT
\<MadFinn\>: call Fiona and ask her
    for ideas
\<BalletGrl\>: I did but she's not
    online and the machine picked up
\<MadFinn\>: I'll call her 18r then
\<BalletGrl\>: Maddie I feel wicked
    awful
\<MadFinn\>: Don't—we'll think of
    something
\<BalletGrl\>: TTFN
\<MadFinn\>: LYLAS

What seemed like a dream concert was now
turning into a nightmare problem! Madison
racked her brain to think of other possible chaperones. But they'd been through this list before. No

one was cool enough or fun enough or anything that would make sense for the Nikki concert—except Roger.

And now he was *busy*.

Phin, who was sitting under Madison's desk, brushed against her leg looking for a little attention. Madison picked him up and looked into his brown pug eyes as she pet his head.

"What'll we do, Phinnie?" she cooed.

Phin purred and snorted back at her, as if to say, "You'll figure it out."

Madison turned off her laptop and opened her history textbook. She had to read chapters 17 and 18 before tomorrow.

Could learning a little about archaeology take her mind off the concert?

Unfortunately, it couldn't.

By the next day, the concert-chaperone problem had still not been solved—and Madison felt even worse about it.

By the middle of Wednesday afternoon, Madison and Fiona had asked everyone they could think of to join them at the concert. Mrs. Waters said she would consider going, but Fiona flatly refused that option. She was afraid her mother would drive everyone crazy. Madison asked Stephanie, since she'd already offered her services willingly, but the date didn't work in Stephanie's schedule. Sadly, she couldn't make it.

How could people have other plans? What was more important than a Nikki concert?

Madison and Fiona stopped by the Gillespie house on the way back from school to break the discouraging news to Aimee.

"Can your parents go?" Fiona asked hopefully.

Aimee got a sadder-than-sad look on her face. She told her BFFs than even *her* mom claimed to be too busy to help out. Unfortunately, Aimee's mom had come down with some feverish stomach flu and couldn't go anywhere for a few days, least of all a hot, stuffy arena.

It was almost Thursday, just forty-eight hours hours shy of their concert date. Hope for finding a new chaperone had dwindled down to a teeny-tiny speck.

"I know what this is," Fiona said in school that Thursday morning. She held up the four concert tickets. "C-O-N-S-P-I-R-A-C-Y," she spelled it out. "Someone wants to keep us from going. I swear my mom put a curse on us."

"We have the tickets and we can't go! Why are we being punished like this?" Aimee cried, grabbing the tickets. "We're in the *front row,* and this is so unfair!"

Madison tried again to convince Fiona that maybe Mrs. Waters would be their best hope for a chaperone, but Fiona still wouldn't hear of it. After all the arguing they'd been through, Fiona was fearful that her mom might ruin everything.

"I know I'm being stupid about it," Fiona explained. "But I just can't go with my mom. I can't. I hope you guys can understand."

Madison wasn't sure she could, but Aimee wrapped her arm around Fiona's shoulder. "It's okay," she said. "We'll find someone else."

Even though Madison didn't really believe Aimee, it was nice to have the old, nongrumpy part of her personality back. She was looking, feeling, and acting better since Monday's accident.

The three of them mingled by the lockers before the first and second bells rang for homeroom, puzzling over any remaining chaperone candidates.

Mr. Gillespie? Had to run the bookstore.

Madison's mom? Date with Paul and his family.

Madison's dad? Out of town.

"Why don't you ask Mrs. Wing?" Fiona suggested to Madison. "Aren't you, like, the teacher's pet?"

"I am not!" Madison said.

"It's not a bad idea," Aimee said. "Mrs. Wing is pretty cool."

"Ask my computer teacher to take us to a concert?" Madison said. "Are you kidding me?"

Mrs. Wing *was* a cooler-than-cool teacher. And her husband ran the animal clinic where Madison volunteered. But that didn't mean Madison wanted them to go with her to a Nikki concert.

How embarrassing.

Just then, Hart and Egg walked past and waved.

Madison turned away a little bit. She was still mad at Hart for liking Carmen.

Following right behind the boys, Poison Ivy Daly appeared from out of a cluster of kids. She was drone-less, carrying her binder and notebooks down the hall toward homeroom. Madison could see that one of the books was plastered with sparkle bumper sticker that read I ❤ NIKKI.

"Hello, Maddie," Ivy grunted as she approached Madison and her friends.

"Oh look," Aimee said. "Our wonderful class president."

Ivy smirked. "Yeah, I am. Got a problem?"

Ivy had been elected class leader at the beginning of the school year in a closer-than-close election. No one was sure how she had won, but she had, and she liked to gloat about it whenever she had the chance. Aimee, of course, liked giving her enemy a hard time about the whole thing whenever she had a chance.

As if Ivy cared. She was already onto the next subject.

"So did I tell you guys that I'm going the Nikki concert tomorrow?" Ivy said.

"Yessss," Aimee hissed.

Madison nudged Fiona as a reminder not to show Ivy the tickets they had for the same concert. Madison still wanted their appearance at the concert to take Ivy by surprise. Catching Ivy off guard was the only way to make her sweat.

"Yeah, you told us about the concert," Madison said.

"Like a hundred times," Aimee added.

"Oh, well, did I mention that I have a pass to meet her? Isn't that cool?" Ivy bragged. "My sister and I do. Janet is taking me."

Madison always wondered how Ivy and Janet could possibly be related. Ivy was a big meanie, while Janet, a senior at Far Hills High School, was nicer than nice. Janet was pretty, too. All the boys wanted to date her.

"Janet says we're like VIP concertgoers," Ivy added for emphasis.

"Yeah, you told us *that* a hundred times, too. No one cares!" Aimee barked.

Fiona giggled.

"What's your problem, Aimee? Hmmm . . . fainted lately?" Ivy said, rolling her eyes.

Aimee didn't respond. Ivy's cruel comment had taken her by surprise. She was still sensitive and embarrassed about not eating and fainting in front of the entire class.

Ivy turned away in a huff and walked down the hall.

Fiona turned to Aimee. "Ivy is a cow," she said. "Mooooo!"

Aimee couldn't help but laugh at that, partly because it sounded funny and partly because Fiona rarely said harsh words about anyone.

"Thanks," Aimee mumbled. "You didn't have to say that."

Madison looked directly at Aimee and Fiona with a beaming look of inspiration on her face.

"What?" Aimee said. She could tell Madison had something very important to say.

"We are so stupid!" Madison said.

"Gee, thanks, Maddie," Aimee said. "That makes me feel so much better."

"No!" Madison said. "I mean we're so stupid about the concert. Our chaperone has been obvious, and we totally missed it."

"What are you talking about, Maddie?" Fiona asked.

"Dean!" Madison said loudly. "Dean is our chaperone. He's perfect!"

"My *brother*, Dean?" Aimee asked.

"It's sooooo obvious," Madison said.

"Really?" Fiona said.

"What are you talking about, Maddie? My brother Dean is a total loser! Why would we want *him* to go with us?" Aimee said.

Brrrring-brrrring.

The homeroom bells echoed through the hall.

Madison grinned. "I have a plan. Meet me after school. You have to trust me. This will work!"

She dashed off to the fourth floor, leaving Fiona and Aimee standing there, scratching their heads.

* * *

A block into their walk home that Thursday afternoon, Madison still had not said anything more about Dean.

Aimee was ready to explode.

"Maddie, are you going to tell us why Dean is the perfect chaperone or what?" Aimee yelled. "Quit playing!"

Madison's grin grew. "I can't believe you guys haven't guessed why he's the one," she said.

Aimee stopped walking. "I am not moving another inch until you tell me."

"Think about Ivy," Madison said. "She's going with her sister Janet . . . who's in high school. . . ."

"Yeah," Aimee said. "So?"

"Aim!" Fiona said. "I get it! Someone from high school can take us."

"So?" Aimee asked.

"Aim," Madison said seriously. "Janet and Dean are the same age. Duh."

Aimee gasped, "I know. But Dean is such a . . ."

"Such a good choice?" Madison grinned.

"Oh, brother, Maddie. He probably won't even go, I swear," Aimee said, hurrying off toward Blueberry Street with her friends. "He's such a pain."

"But he's our last chance!" Fiona said, running ahead of her friends.

Madison and Aimee laughed.

When they arrived at the Gillespie house, the

threesome was lucky enough to find Dean sitting in the living room like a lump, watching TV. They cornered him immediately.

"What do you three want?" Dean grunted.

"Dean," Aimee said in her sweetest voice ever, "we were wondering . . ."

". . . since Roger can't take us to the Nikki concert anymore . . ." Madison continued.

"Will you take us? Please?" Aimee finished.

"I'm not going to your idiot concert, Aim," Dean said. "Leave me alone."

The three sighed. This would take some serious begging. Aimee tried to offer him her allowance money, but he said no. She also offered to do all his house chores for a month, but he said no to that, too.

"Nikki stinks," Dean said, turning up the volume on the TV. "She has a cute belly button, but I hate her music. She can't sing."

Madison sat next to Dean and re-explained the seriousness of the situation—how they had won the tickets, how it was the opportunity of a lifetime, and how they absolutely had to go to the concert because their enemy Poison Ivy Daly was going to be there with her sister Janet.

"You'd be saving us," Madison said.

Aimee sat on the couch wringing her hands. "Dean, will you just please do this . . . *Please*?"

Dean gave his sister a blank stare, as usual. Then

he turned to Madison and said, "Wait a minute. Did you say Janet *Daly*?"

"Yes," Madison said.

He smiled. "Are you saying that if I took you guys to the concert I could hang with Janet Daly?"

"Totally," Madison said quickly without thinking.

Fiona shot her a look. "Maddie . . ."

"Who cares about Janet Daly?" Aimee asked.

"If we can hang with Janet, then I'll go," Dean said, without another pause. "I've been trying to get a date with Janet Daly all year."

"A date?" Madison said.

Fiona gulped.

Aimee's jaw dropped.

Yes, they'd be able to go to the concert, but Madison couldn't help but wonder if she'd made a terrible mistake. Dean was practically drooling at the idea of hanging out with Janet Daly, which was gross enough. But hanging with Janet meant they'd be hanging out with Poison Ivy, too.

And *that* was grosser than gross.

Chapter 11

 Nikki

Rude Awakening: Now that it's time to face the music, it's time to face the enemy, too.

HELP!

How could I have said all those dumber-than-dumb things to Dean? I wanted to go to this concert so badly that I completely spaced out on the reality of what I was saying. Spend the whole night with Ivy? HELP! Even Fiona realized what was happening. Aimee wanted to kick me. She still does.

Tonight we will be standing at the concert for real. Will it be awful standing near HER? Fiona says that at least Ivy's in the fifth row and we're up front. She'll be jealous of US for a change, right?

I will try not to obsess about this. The most important thing is that we're going—after everything that has happened—we are going to our very first concert! Seeing Nikki is a dream come true for all of us.

Only twelve more hours until we're there.

Madison closed her laptop file. She'd woken up Friday morning thinking about a lot of different things: her self-portrait for art class (which was due today), an English vocabulary quiz she was doomed to flunk (she hadn't studied), and, of course, Nikki.

Nikki, Nikki, Nikki.

Could Madison survive just one more day of school before the concert?

Aimee had her dance lesson that morning—the first one since she'd fainted earlier in the week—so Madison walked to school alone. When she arrived by the lockers, Madison couldn't find Fiona or anyone else to talk to. A bunch of other seventh graders passed by wearing Nikki buttons. Madison kept her eyes open for Ivy, the one person she absolutely did not want to see.

In her rush to get her books and dash down the hall, however, she nearly collided with the one other person she dreaded seeing.

Carmen.

"Hey, Madison," Carmen said, acting friendly for the first time that Madison could remember. "Is that your picture for Mr. Duane?" she asked.

Madison toted a rolled-up piece of art wrapped with a rubber band. She looked down at the scroll and then up at Carmen.

"Yeah," Madison mumbled. "I'm bringing it to Hart class."

Carmen giggled. "You're what?"

Madison felt her cheeks get hot. *Hart* class? "I mean *art* class," Madison said.

Carmen nodded with a smile. "I know what you mean."

The desire to run surged through Madison's body, but she couldn't move. She stared blankly at Carmen and cursed her lead feet.

"Did you like our self-portrait assignment?" Carmen asked.

Why was she still standing there? Madison couldn't believe Carmen wanted to talk more. She couldn't carry on a conversation now! Not this morning!

Carmen kept talking, though. "I thought it was hard. I don't really like staring at myself in the mirror, you know? It's so vain."

"Yeah," Madison said. She didn't say much more.

"Well, I have to go," Carmen said, taking off in the opposite direction. "Maybe I'll see you later."

Madison heaved a sigh of relief when Carmen

walked away, but her embarrassment only increased the more Madison thought about the exchange.

Hart class?

Between Dean yesterday and Carmen this morning, Madison was beginning to wonder why the censor between her brain and her mouth had quit working. And now, to make matters worse, Carmen had to suspect Madison's true feelings for Hart Jones, right? Why else would she have said something as stupid as *Hart class?*

Madison wandered off to her English section, head swimming with thoughts of Nikki, Hart, and a vocabulary list she could barely recall.

So far, the day of the concert was not turning out the way she'd hoped.

When the last class bell of the day rang out in the halls of Far Hills Junior High, Madison nearly screamed aloud. Her pulse raced. Her chest pounded. She even felt a little dizzy.

Only five more hours until THE CONCERT.

Luckily, Madison didn't have to look very far to find her BFFs. Aimee and Fiona were waiting in the hall by the lockers, bubbling over with just as much nervous energy and excitement as she was.

"Oh my GOD!" Aimee squealed. "I can't believe it's here!"

"Me neither," Fiona giggled. "What are you guys going to wear?"

"I am definitely wearing my moonstone earrings," Madison said. Dad had given them to her, and they always brought good luck. Madison wanted to make sure that everything about this concert-going experience was good *and* lucky.

"I am wearing those pink pants I bought at the mall last week, my Nikki T-shirt, and . . ." Aimee said, taking a deep breath, "this brand-new jean jacket with this big heart patch on it."

Aimee pulled the jacket out of her locker. "My mom gave it to me before dance this morning. Isn't it awesome?"

"Hey," Fiona said. "You're so . . . coordinated."

"You're always coordinated, Aim," Madison said.

"I know," Aimee said, smiling. She was back to her old self again.

The three friends packed up their bags and headed home. They made arrangements to meet up at six o'clock. Dean was going to pick up Madison and Fiona after they ate dinner at home and had a chance to get dressed up for Nikki. The concert arena was located only a short drive from downtown Far Hills. They could get there early enough to buy souvenirs and grab their seats.

Madison bounced inside when she got home. Phinnie knew something was up—he could always tell when Madison was energized about something. Phin would get energized, too. He jumped up onto her lap as soon as she sat down, licking her face all over.

"Phin! Stop! STOP!" Madison pleaded. "I'm going to have doggy slobber all over me."

Mom, who was working in her home office, came into the hall to say hello.

"Well, someone's excited," she said, grabbing Phin's collar so Madison could get away from his drool.

"Yeah," Madison sputtered. "Gross me."

"How are you doing?" Mom asked.

Madison mumbled "Fine" as she wiped her mouth.

"I'm making soup and sandwiches for supper," Mom said. "So we'll eat around five-thirty, okay?"

Madison slung her orange bag over her shoulder and headed toward the stairs. "Okay," she said.

"Hey! What's going on? Aren't you excited?" Mom called out. "You've only been looking forward to this concert for two weeks now. You've barely said two words to me since you walked in the front door."

"Of course, I'm excited!" Madison said, turning around on the stairs. "Oh, Mom, I just don't know what to wear, as usual. And I want tonight to be greater than great. I can't believe I'm actually going to meet Nikki."

Mom shook her head. "I know, honey bear. It's a big deal."

"I'll be in my room," Madison said, bounding up the stairs. She didn't have time to chat with Mom now. There were far more important tasks to accomplish.

Like checking in with her keypal, Bigwheels.

Madison always went to her for advice about school and friends, and now she needed help with fashion.

What would Bigwheels wear to the most important concert of her life?

Unfortunately, it was only four o'clock, and Bigwheels was all the way across the country, which meant that Insta-Messaging probably wouldn't work right now. Bigwheels was still in classes or at lunch, not home on the computer, like Madison.

Madison opened a new file.

 Picture-Perfect

Rude Awakening: Looks are definitely not everything.

What's the point of fashion crazes when all they do is make me CRAZY! Every time I try to dress cool . . . I look lukewarm. Where's Aimee when I need her? Where's Bigwheels?

I have to look picture-perfect at this concert.

Everyone else will. I don't want to be left out.

Madison stopped typing and stared into her closet. She still didn't have a solution to her fashion angst by the time she was through ranting. She still didn't know what to wear!

Before logging off, she checked her buddy list one last time just to make sure her keypal hadn't sneaked online since before.

Of course, she hadn't.

But thankfully, someone else had.

```
<Wetwinz>: Maddie!
<MadFinn>: Fiona!
<Wetwinz>: I'm sooo glad ur online
    I was gonna call u
<MadFinn>: me 2!!!!!!!!
<Wetwinz>: I dunno what 2 wear esp.
    after Aim was so sure of her
    clothes WHAT r u wearing? I need
    HELP!
<MadFinn>: GMTA I need mega help 2
<Wetwinz>: LOL
<MadFinn>: u should wear that blue
    belly shirt
<Wetwinz>: w/my jeans?
<MadFinn>: TOTALLY
<Wetwinz>: well I know this sounds
    weird but u should wear what u had
    on @ school 2day u looked cute
<MadFinn>: &'''-1
<Wetwinz>: fine! What about ur gray
    baseball shirt?
<MadFinn>: &'''-1
<Wetwinz>: ok then wear the orange
    tee with the kitty on it u know
    the one I love
```

```
<MadFinn>: I forgot about that shirt
    what a great idea!
<Wetwinz>: and wear ur patchwork
    jeans since they are way cool
<MadFinn>: TX sooo much
<Wetwinz>: YW!
<MadFinn>: BTW how r u wearing ur
    hair?
<Wetwinz>: same braids as always in
    my blue headband
<MadFinn>: I think I'll wear mine
    down BYE!
<Wetwinz>: CWYL
<MadFinn>: *poof*
```

Madison had to dig through all her drawers and closet before she located the orange kitty shirt. It had shrunk since it was last washed, so it rode up a little on her stomach, but Madison didn't mind. It did look good with her patchwork jeans, too. Fiona had been right. And the moonstone earrings matched perfectly.

Once dressed, Madison stared at her reflection in the bathroom mirror for more than ten minutes before deciding on the perfect 'do. She wore her hair back in little kitty clips that Gramma Helen had bought her last year. Just like Aimee, Madison was (at last!) super-coordinated—or at least she hoped so.

She glanced at the clock.

It was flashing a digital blue 5:12.

Only three more hours until THE CONCERT.

"Maddie," Mom yelled from downstairs. "I want you to come and eat now. Aren't your friends coming to get you in half an hour?"

Madison patted body glitter powder onto her arms and neck and cheeks and grabbed her tub of strawberry-kiwi lip gloss. She'd reapply more gloss after eating. Then she shoved those things, tissues, her wallet, and an extra kitty clip into her small purse. The purse was sewn from Indian fabric that shimmered with teeny mirrors all over. She'd only used it once, but never for a special occasion like this. Madison zipped it shut and looked at her reflection in the mirror one last time.

Standing there, Madison realized that she saw something very different in that mirror—different than what she had seen the other night while working on her art class assignment. The "self-portrait" in front of her right now wasn't as awful as she'd thought before. She even felt a little pretty, shimmering with the glitter powder, her hair framing her face.

And the evil zit had practically disappeared.

She wasn't sure why, but feeling good made her look good.

Happiness was what was pretty.

"Maddie!" Mom yelled again. "I said get down here and eat and I mean it! Now!"

Madison was jolted from her thoughts. "I'm coming, I'm coming!" she yelled back, turning off her light and heading for the stairs.

Mom had dinner set out. Madison only managed to slurp down a cup of soup and half a sandwich before the doorbell rang.

Mom grinned. "Well, there's Aimee," she said.

"Oh, wow! I am psyched," Madison said, standing up from the dinner table. "This is the best night of my life so far."

"You look very beautiful," Mom said. "I'm sure the three of you will have a great time together. Give me a kiss, will you?"

Madison hugged her mom and headed for the door. Phin followed, but Madison didn't let his little paws or his slobber near this oufit. She petted him on the head instead, and made her clean getaway.

Outside, Aimee was waiting on the front porch, jumping up and down.

"Oh my God I feel like I'm going to explode like a stack of dynamite or something!" Aimee said. "Hurry up and let's go get Fiona!"

The two friends waved back to Mom, who was now standing on the Finn porch holding Phin in her arms.

Dean honked the horn. "Let's go!" he said.

Madison and Aimee squealed with anticipation. They really were headed to their first concert!

Chapter 12

Mrs. Waters waved to the car as Fiona got inside. She still looked unsure about her decision to let the trio go to the concert, but it was too late.

They were on their way.

Much to everyone's disappointment, Dean spent the entire ride over to the concert arena talking about Poison Ivy's sister. Aimee, sitting next to her brother in the front seat, looked ready to slug him every time the words *Janet Daly* came out of his mouth.

Madison and Fiona tried to help make Aimee feel better by changing the subject, but it didn't do much good. Aimee seemed determined to be mad at her brother, no matter what he said. She pasted on a superpout and stared blankly out the window.

Was the sweetest concert in the world already going sour?

"Aim?" Madison asked from the backseat. "Are you feeling okay?"

"Huh?" Aimee said. "Of course! Why are you asking me that? Don't I look okay?" Even though she had recovered from her fainting episode, she was still a little touchy about the whole subject of feelings.

"You look great!" Madison said. "I just wanted to make sure."

"Do you think I look okay, Fiona?" Aimee asked.

Fiona nodded. "Absolutely."

Dean chuckled. "Yeah, for a toady little sister," he said under his breath.

Aimee hauled off and punched him in the shoulder. Madison had tried to turn down some of the front-seat heat between them, but instead, she'd made Aimee a little angrier at her brother. Dean screamed. Aimee screamed back.

"You're the toad!" Aimee shouted.

"Why don't you cool out!" Dean said. "I'm the one doing you a favor here."

"Toad!" Aimee yelled again.

Their fight got louder . . . and louder . . . and louder. . . .

"Look!" Madison said, pointing. She had to find some way to put a chill on the fighting. "Over there!"

Everyone in the car turned to see the neon signs welcoming cars into the Far Hills Concert Arena. There was a long line of traffic pulling into the parking areas. Dean honked his horn a few times, which annoyed Aimee, but she didn't yell anymore. Madison's distraction tactic had worked. Now all the girls could focus on was the activity going into the concert. They glanced into other cars to see what other girls were wearing; they searched the parking lot for people they might know; and they looked high and low for the truck and the stand for WKBM Radio. With their radio-won tickets, they were allowed to go collect an exclusive Nikki iron-on patch for each of them.

Dean parked the car about a mile away from the gates, or at least it seemed that far. Aimee looked ready to pounce on him again for doing the "wrong" thing, but Madison distracted her once more with talk of Nikki.

The concert was only ONE hour away.

Dean looked around too. "This is a bunch of little kids," he groaned. "I can't believe I let you three talk me into coming here."

"Do you see Ivy anywhere?" Fiona asked as they walked toward the stadium.

"Yeah, Dean. Don't forget about Janet," Aimee joked. "I'm so sure she's dying to see you."

"She will be," Dean bragged. He had the biggest ego of any boy Madison had ever known. According to Aimee, Dean had already dated half his senior class. Finding new girlfriends was like a game for him. Tonight he was on the prowl for Janet.

"Oh, no!" Fiona said a moment later. "There they are."

Madison, Aimee, and Fiona turned at the exact same time to see Ivy and Janet walking toward the arena, too. Ivy was wearing tight-fitting pants and a teeny little top with spaghetti straps. Janet had on a sweatshirt.

"Isn't Ivy cold?" Aimee asked. "I mean, she's wearing practically nothing. And that shirt and pants are so uncoordinated."

Madison sighed. Coordinated or not, it worked. Ivy looked good in practically nothing. Madison wondered briefly if "practically nothing" was prettier than her orange kitty shirt. Probably. All at once, Madison's earlier happiness faded a teeny bit.

"You're so much prettier than her," Fiona said to Madison, wrapping her arm around Madison's shoulder.

Madison leaned into Fiona. "Thanks," she said, hip-checking her BFF.

"So let's go get 'em," Dean yelled, making his move diagonally across the parking lot. "What are you three waiting for?"

Aimee moaned. "Dean! Noooo!" But it was no use. He was halfway to Janet already. Madison wondered what Ivy's older sister would really think about

Aimee's brother once he walked right up to her. Would she laugh in his face? Or maybe she did like him a little bit?

The three BFFs hustled across the parking lot in pursuit of Dean. He made it to the Daly sisters before they could.

"Yo! Janet!" Dean said, nodding his head. "You look great. What are you doing here?"

"Dean Gillespie?" Janet said. "What are you doing here?"

"I know what he's doing here," Ivy moaned. She'd caught sight of Madison, Aimee, and Fiona. "He's with them."

Janet turned to see the three friends approach. "Maddie!" she cried out.

Back in the third-grade days when Ivy and Madison had been best of elementary-school friends, Madison had also taken a super shine to Ivy's sister. Janet was a different kind of person from Poison Ivy. She wasn't poisonous in the least. She had always been nice to Madison when her parents were fighting, as they used to do a lot before the Big D.

"So," Ivy said. "What *are* you three doing here?"

Fiona smiled. "We won tickets on the radio." She could finally say it now that they were here in the flesh.

"Yeah, we won tickets in the front row. Imagine that?" Madison said.

Ivy snickered. "Yeah, right. Let me see."

"Um, I don't think so," Aimee butted in. "We have to be going now."

Dean and Janet were standing a little off to the side talking. Madison realized that they were talking *nicely*, which wasn't a good sign. Now she was fearful that they really would be hanging with the enemy all night long.

"Dean!" Aimee yelled. "We want to go sit down now."

Dean looked at Janet and shrugged. "I ll see you inside I guess," Dean said.

Janet tilted her head forward a little bit. "Yeah. When everyone goes into the aisles to dance. I'll see you then."

Madison sighed to herself. They were making plans to meet up inside? She grabbed Fiona's arm and tugged her toward a souvenir stand.

"Can we please go inside, now?" Madison said.

Aimee agreed. She grabbed her brother's arm. "Later for you," Aimee said to Ivy.

Ivy just snarled. "Much later," she said.

Unfortunately, Madison knew that wasn't exactly the way it would play.

Inside the arena, people were swarming in and around each other like insects. Everywhere the eye could see, pictures of Nikki smiled down upon the crowds from T-shirts, posters, television monitors playing music videos, and other memorabilia.

Madison couldn't believe how many people were crammed around the food-and-beverage stand. Girls had painted their faces with stars over one eye, a look that Nikki used on one of her most popular posters. The theme of this concert appeared to be "Circus." There were dozens of belly shirts and jean jackets, but Madison was glad to see not one other girl wearing her orange kitty T-shirt. Clowns wandered in and around the concession area.

"Let's get a program," Aimee shouted at her brother Dean. "Over there!"

Reluctantly, Dean followed the three girls over to an area where two ultratall workers passed out souvenir guides from atop stilts. The program cost Madison, Fiona, and Aimee their allowances combined.

To the left, ticket takers bellowed, "Step right up!" and welcomed concertgoers inside the main doors to the arena. One was wearing a tuxedo with a purple-and-yellow feathered hat.

Madison wasn't sure she liked all the noise, but it was the most exciting place she'd ever been—more exciting than a soccer game at school or a local league baseball showdown with Dad and Stephanie. She screamed right along with everyone else, including her BFFs.

"This . . . is . . . to die for!" Fiona said, straining her voice above the din.

"Step right up! Nikki performing in the center ring!" the tuxedo man said.

137

"Nice feathers." Dean cracked up as they passed through the gates.

Someone shoved Madison, and she crashed into Fiona, who didn't mind. Aimee was quick—and happy—to point out that by now they'd lost track of Ivy and her sister Janet.

"Hurry up, you guys," Aimee urged them on. "I see the door for our ticket numbers up ahead— B30."

Their gate was the main gate, so things got even more squished from there. Hundreds of screaming fans were pressing inside two wide doors, and there still wasn't enough room for everyone.

Madison, Fiona, and Aimee grabbed hands as they stepped through into the arena.

"Wow!" Madison said as she looked around. There were people, people, everywhere as far as the eye could see. It was larger than life, just as she'd imagined it would be. She could hear voices coming from every corner. She could smell popcorn and per-fumes mixed together. The entire room was a blur of colored T-shirts, giggling girls, and posters that read NIKKI WE LOVE YOU.

Aimee was still leading the way. "Over here!" she called out, tugging on Fiona's hand. Fiona tugged on Madison, too.

Dean was frantically searching the sea of faces for Janet.

"Wait a minute!" Aimee said as they approached

their seating area. "There are no seats. No chairs!"

Aimee was right. Madison and Fiona glanced around. The entire area in front of the stage was "open seating," a second usher said, urging the girls to move it along. WKBM had set it up this way on purpose. The front section was meant to be a large dance area. Someone would be shooting a video of the concert and wanted lots of fans screaming and dancing in front.

"Bummer," Fiona said.

Madison agreed, mostly because she had caught view of someone else by now. Ivy was standing just a few yards away. The enemy waved.

"So I guess we have the same seats after all," Ivy boasted with a smirk.

When Dean hustled over to stand next to Janet, Madison knew the truth.

They weren't moving from that spot. By now the throng of other ticket holders had been pushed into the small area so there was nowhere left to go except right where they were standing.

Madison turned to Fiona and whispered, "This isn't really what I expected."

Fiona nodded. "Me, neither. But at least we're here."

Aimee wasn't saying much. She'd been distracted by something up ahead. Some belly dancers had come out into the circus setup onstage, and she was watching them intently as they pranced around in exotic veils. Some large man was leading a camel on the side of the stage.

After several elbows to the side and a few more evil sidelong glances from Ivy, Madison was relieved when the concert lights finally started to flicker and then dim completely. A hush and sigh went over the crowd. Kids all over squealed and whistled. It was hotter than hot, but Madison's pulse was racing with delight.

The concert was HERE.

The music started up slowly at first, with the tinkle of little bells and a sound like wind. Madison felt her feet lift up ever so slightly off the floor. She wanted to see and feel everything that happened.

"BEEEE my LUV ma-SHEEN!"

A group of dancers all in black rushed the front of the stage, right near where Madison and the rest were standing. They each slid in on one knee, as if they might slide right off the stage.

A microphone boomed, and the chorus sang out the lyrics to one of Nikki's most popular songs: "Be my love machine!"

In a ball of colored light, an elevator came down from the ceiling in the center of the stage. Smoke billowed around it like clouds. Dean whispered something to Madison and Aimee about how that was dry ice that caused the special effect. Madison was captivated by its rainbow of light; she waited breathlessly to see what would happen next.

POW!

All at once, the doors to the elevator blew open, and out of a cloud of colored smoke came Nikki.

"Ooooooh!" Aimee wailed. "She looks perfect!"

Ivy was jumping up and down by now, too.

"BEEEE my LUV ma-SHEEN! You're the cutest boy I've ever seeeeen!"

The entire arena screamed. Madison and her friends tried to sing along, but they were too stunned by the flash and the noise to keep up.

As Nikki danced around the stage, Aimee oohed and ahhed. Nikki changed costumes eight times; rode around the stage on an elephant; and sang every song the girls loved, from "Take Me There" to "Living on the Edge of Y-O-U," to "Download My Heart."

Madison wanted to hear "Sugar-Sweet (Like You)," her favorite Nikki tune, but Nikki didn't sing it. And too soon, it seemed that she was singing the finale. It was like fireworks in the arena. The stage show even had a man shot out of a cannon—or at least it looked that way.

"What about 'Sugar Sweet'?" Madison whispered to her friends.

Ivy heard. "Maddie, it's probably her encore. I mean, that is her number-one hit right now. Don't they always play that for the encore?"

Madison didn't know that the encore was a definite thing, but Dean explained that usually stars saved fan favorites for the very, very end.

Sure enough, as soon as Nikki had played her "last" song, the crowd roared with applause and then began clapping and chanting.

"SUGAR-SWEET! SUGAR-SWEET!"

Madison, Fiona, and Aimee chanted right along with them.

The room went dark for just a moment, and then a squeaky electronic noise filled the arena. Everyone had to block his and her ears for a moment. Then, a computerized robot voice came on the loudspeaker.

"Step right up!" the voice said. "The amazing, the astounding, NIKKI!"

The crowd cheered as Nikki pranced back onstage, microphone in hand. "I could be sugar-sweet like you. Sugar, sugar-sweet . . ."

Madison squealed as loudly as she could. Ivy did, too. In one fleeting moment, they were smiling at the same time, bopping up and down, singing along with their favorite superstar in the whole world.

It was a picture-perfect moment.

Chapter 13

The chorus of "Sugar-Sweet" went on and on for ten minutes. Some girls in the crowd were actually crying, they were so happy to see the number-one song being performed live.

No one wanted the moment to stop. Except maybe Dean. He jokingly covered his ears, which made Janet laugh.

As the final, *final* applause started up, Madison and Fiona gave each other a huge hug. Aimee threw her arms around the two of them.

They had made it to the concert. And it was a roaring success.

Off to the side, Ivy stood alone, looking around the room. Madison realized that the fleeting moment of bonding she and Ivy had shared had passed once again. Ivy was still poisonous; not even a sweet song could change that.

Large numbers of people began to file out of the arena. One of the people dressed up as a clown stepped up to one of the microphones onstage and called for everyone's attention in the front section. He was in charge of getting the designated concert-goers backstage for their meet-and-greet with Nikki.

Madison, Fiona, and Aimee were ready to faint when they heard that. This was the moment they'd really been waiting for.

Ivy tugged on her sister's arm. "Can we go? Can we?" Ivy begged.

Janet shrugged. "I don't know if we can with our tickets," she said. "I think it's just for these guys. We should get home."

Madison wanted to shout out "Ha!" but she didn't rub it in.

Ivy looked away.

Dean frowned. "So you guys are gonna take off then?" he asked Janet.

They whispered back and forth to each other for another minute or so while the rest of the group just stood there like zombies.

Then, in the blink of an eye, Janet and Ivy turned to walk out. Ivy didn't say anything else. Their part of the concert was over. And she was out.

Dean gave Janet a high-five sign, as if to say, "See you later." Madison could tell they probably would

144

be going on a date sooner than soon. She briefly wondered how seniors in high school like them could make a date and decide to like each other so quickly. Why didn't that work for her and . . . Hart?

"Step right up!" a funny-looking man yelled to the radio winners. It was Stevie Steves, the radio announcer from WKBM. Madison recognized his voice.

Madison and her BFFs linked arms and followed Dean and the rest of the group toward the backstage area. They climbed up a little staircase onto the stage itself and then moved back toward huge black curtains.

Madison noticed that the floor of the stage was covered with tape marks and numbers and little trap doors—all the stuff she couldn't see from out front, not even from the front row. The air was hot and smoky from the concert. Round, white-hot bulbs circled the front of the stage. Madison noticed that it was almost impossible to see anything in the audience beyond the footlights.

The entryway to the official "backstage area," was nothing spectacular. Unlike the exciting circus setup out front, backstage was merely a mess of clothes piled here and a cluster of wires stretched there. Everything was crammed in together with little room for moving around. But then the group was led into a slightly larger space for refreshments. That was more impressive.

Madison and her friends lingered by a food table and Dean poured himself a cup of punch. All over the walls in the room were concert posters of Nikki; a giant WKBM banner; and multicolored helium balloons that read NIKKI'S SUGAR-SWEET on them. In one corner, there was a popcorn machine, and in the other, a cotton-candy maker. The circus theme continued.

"I can't believe we're backstage," Fiona said, her voice squeaking.

"This is awesome," Aimee said.

"I think it's a little weird," Madison mumbled to herself. "Cool, but weird."

She was looking around at the crew of people assembled backstage. On one side of the room was a group of screaming girls just like them; and on the other side of the room was another group of screaming girls just like them.

Everyone seemed the same.

One girl looked gray, as if she might faint. "She looks like I did last week," Aimee said.

"I'm so glad you got better, Aim," Fiona said.

"I wouldn't have missed this for anything," Aimee said.

Madison leaned on Aimee's shoulder. "I'm glad," she said.

From across the room, two beefy security guards opened a side door, and a cluster of bodies moved into the room. Behind them, Madison and the rest saw a short, blond girl approach.

It was Nikki. Live.

"Attention, everyone!" Stevie Steves called out to the hundred or so people who were stuffed together in the room. "Presenting the star of tonight's show, Nikki!"

The room burst into applause. Madison clapped as loudly as anyone.

Dean was so busy scoping out other cute girls in the room that he barely noticed Nikki's arrival. When Aimee grabbed him to point to the singing star, he just shrugged.

"What's the big deal?" he said. "I mean, she's okay onstage, but I don't think she's that pretty."

A stranger standing next to Dean made a face and told him to shut up, but he didn't care. He went back over to the punch bowl for another drink.

"Look at her hair!" Aimee said. "Just like in the magazine."

"Well," Fiona said. "Look closer. You can tell she's not a real blond. Look at the top."

Aimee sounded disappointed. "Really? I guess you're right."

"She's shorter than I thought," Madison said.

"I agree with Dean," Fiona whispered. "She isn't that pretty. Do you guys think she is?"

"Of course we do!" Aimee said, laughing, as if Fiona were joking around.

But Madison knew that Fiona was serious.

Nikki walked over toward them, barely waving

hello to the many fans who were trying to stop her along the way. She wanted something to drink and ordered one of her assistants to get her a juice on ice.

"Make sure it has three cubes," Nikki said. "I want it cold."

By now, the star was standing only a few feet away from Madison and her friends. She turned to look around the room and nearly slammed into Aimee.

"Um, excuse me," Nikki said. "Do you mind?"

"Oh, I'm sorry," Aimee said. She reached out for Nikki's arm as if to say, "Are you okay?"

"Um, don't touch, 'kay?" Nikki said, pulling her arm back. She smirked and walked off in the other direction.

Aimee turned around as if she'd just been slapped.

"That was so rude," Fiona said. "She is so not what I expected."

"Weird," Madison said again. "This whole thing is so weird."

Despite the rudeness, everything about being backstage was a thrill. Standing around with record producers and other fans, drinking punch, and even watching Nikki act the super pop-star diva was fun.

"So do we just stand around and watch Her Highness all night?" Fiona said. "I'm wicked disappointed."

Madison sighed. "I know what you mean, but I'm not ready to leave yet, are you?"

They all glanced over at Dean, who had taken a seat by the refreshments and was chatting with one of the security guys.

"My brother even found someone to talk to," Aimee said.

"I wish she would just come and talk with some of us," Fiona said. "Let's go over to Nikki and ask her a question."

Madison froze. She didn't know what question to ask.

Aimee didn't know either.

So Fiona didn't move.

A few moments later, Nikki made her way back over toward their side of the room. The three friends just stared at her every move. It seemed that she was finally making her rounds, shaking hands and meeting her fans up close. She was smiling now, too.

"Maybe she was only mean and crabby before because she'd just finished up her show," Aimee said, making excuses for the star.

"Maybe," Fiona said.

Madison wasn't so sure.

As Nikki walked over, Madison looked her squarely in the eye to see if she could get a sense of what this person was *really* like. She remembered something Gramma Helen always said about not judging a book by its cover. Is that what Madison and her friends had done with Nikki—but only in reverse? They'd looked at her picture-perfect posing in *Teen Blast* magazine and assumed that Nikki was the same kind of person on the inside.

But she wasn't. Not by a long shot.

Nikki sidled up to Madison, Aimee, and Fiona and asked them if they'd won their tickets on the radio. Everyone nodded in sync, no one saying much more than a mumbled *yeah* or *nah* to Nikki's questions.

Madison leaned forward a little as they were talking, still searching for something nice. As she stared, Nikki kept glancing away. She sighed a lot, too, as if she had somewhere better to be.

Not only that, but she had a few spots on her face. Madison could see that she had put on tons of stage makeup for her show, and much of it had been sweated off and powdered back on again. Her skin looked bumpy all over.

Nikki had zits. Lots of zits.

While they were standing there, Dean came over to shake Nikki's hand.

Nikki bowed her head and giggled when he did that. "Who are you?" she asked coyly, tossing her hair in the air.

"Is she flirting with my brother?" Aimee whispered to Madison and Fiona.

Dean didn't smile much or say much. He really wasn't impressed. Instead he asked, "So, what's with the clowns and the guys in feather hats?" he asked.

Nikki frowned. "Excuse me?"

"The whole circus thing is a little freaky," Dean said. "Dontcha think?"

One of Nikki's assistants who was standing by heard that and gently began to lead Nikki away from them.

Meanwhile, Nikki's next group of fans squealed and gushed all over. Nikki needed adoration. Dean wasn't about to give her one ounce of the stuff.

"She does work really hard," Fiona said, trying to see both sides of the situation and be fair. "That counts for a lot, right?"

"Yeah, but that doesn't give her a reason not to be nice, does it?" Madison asked her friends.

Aimee sighed. "What a letdown."

"She isn't as smart as I thought," Fiona said.

"Let's blow this Popsicle stand," Dean said. "Later for the plastic music queen."

The three friends took one last look at their idol and then followed Aimee's brother out the backstage sidedoor.

The ride back home in Dean's car took the edge off the backstage experience. Despite Nikki's less-than-perfect demeanor, the concert itself had been worthwhile. Everyone agreed that the elephant was one of the most exciting parts.

"She has so many fans!" Aimee said. "Can you imagine what it's like having that many people who want your autograph or want to talk to you?"

Madison stared out the window, lost in thought. No, the evening had not been everything she'd dreamed, but it had been the experience of a lifetime. She wondered what Ivy would have said to Nikki if they'd had a run-in in the backstage area. Would Ivy have considered the star a big poser, too?

Somewhere along the way home, Aimee started humming "Sugar-Sweet," and Madison and Fiona joined in. They were bouncing together as they sang the chorus.

"So, Dean," Aimee asked her brother as they drove along. "What's the deal with Janet?"

He smiled. "Got her digits."

Fiona made a spaced-out face. "Huh? What's that?"

"Phone number!" Aimee said. "So are you going to ask her out, Dean?"

Madison and Fiona giggled.

Dean nodded seriously. "I'm calling her tomorrow."

"What do you think makes a girl pretty?" Madison asked Dean out of the blue. He seemed a little taken aback.

"Pretty . . . I have no clue," Dean said.

"Yeah you do," Aimee pleaded. "Is it a cool 'do or nice eyes or smarts or what?"

"She has to be nice," Dean said, glancing over at his sister but keeping his eyes on the road.

The car fell silent. All ears were on Dean. After all, he was the guy who could get dates with girls in three minutes.

Dean shrugged and stared straight ahead. "I really don't see the big deal about that Nikki chick," he said. "That's why you guys are asking, right? I mean, you three are way prettier than she could ever be."

Aimee let out a little gasp. Then she punched her brother right in the shoulder.

"What was that for?" Dean yelped.

Aimee turned around and looked at her friends. They all laughed.

"You are such a liar," Aimee said.

"Whatever," Dean said, rolling his eyes. Madison could see him do that in the rearview mirror.

Despite all of its ups and downs, none of them wanted this night to end.

Chapter 14

"So tell me everything and don't leave out a single moment," Mom said to Madison as soon as she'd walked in the front door.

Madison grinned. "It was so cool, Mom. The people, the arena—they had this circus theme—and the singing and there was a real live elephant on stage, too."

"An elephant?" Mom asked.

"Yup," Madison said. "And clowns, and a guy on stilts, and a ringmaster like in a real circus."

"So what was Nikki like? Was she a good dancer and singer?" Mom asked.

Madison yawned. "She was okay."

"Okay?" Mom said. She sounded a little surprised. "I thought she was the greatest singer ever. She was, yesterday."

"Yeah, well . . ." Madison's voice drifted off.

"I think maybe it's time for you to hit the hay," Mom said, putting her arm over Madison's shoulder. "Phin and I have been waiting up for you, but we're pretty sleepy, too."

"Roworrrrooooo!" Phin wailed as soon as he heard his name. Madison bent down to scratch the tip-top of his head.

"Your dad called tonight," Mom said as she tucked Madison into bed a few moments later. "He wanted to say he was thinking of you at your first concert. We both were. It was a big night, Maddie."

"It sure was," Madison said.

"Good night, honey bear," Mom said before shutting off the overhead light. Phin jumped up onto Madison's bed and snuggled into her side.

"Good night, Mom," Madison said.

She closed her eyes and thought of Nikki dancing in rainbow light and smoke onstage. Nothing could take that excitement away from Madison, not even Nikki's crummy attitude. The concert was seared into her memory forever.

And she'd shared it all with her best friends in the whole world.

The next morning, Madison got up very late. Mom let her sleep until after eleven o'clock! The first thing she did after jumping out of bed was to log onto her laptop. Bigwheels would be expecting an e-mail update on the concert. So would Dad. She was off to a late start!

She reopened her Nikki file first.

 Nikki

It was funny standing next to Ivy of all people while we were at the concert last night. I always thought she was the fakest person I knew, but now I've met someone even worse—Nikki.

Rude Awakening: Nothing is as pretty as a picture.

Teen Blast is a big lie. Fiona was right all along. She is so smart sometimes. They DO airbrush pictures in that magazine. That's why I never saw that Nikki has zits just like me. I never saw a lot of things.

It was hard for Madison to keep her mind on writing in her files when her e-mailbox was full. She scrolled down and picked out the e-mails she wanted to read and respond to now. She'd save the rest for later.

FROM	SUBJECT
✉ FHASC	Clinic Update: Beagle-Mania
✉ Go Nikki!	Sugar-Sweet Nikki News
✉ JeffFinn	Dinner?
✉ Wetwinz	LYLAS
✉ BalletGrl	Re: LYLAS
✉ Bigwheels	Write Back Soon

The day before, the Far Hills Clinic had sent an update about new adoptable dogs. This time, the announcement was about a litter of baby beagles that had been born to an abandoned dog. The clinic wanted to help place the puppies into new homes. Madison considered asking Mom if they could get a second dog, but she knew the answer would be no. They had enough to deal with Phin. He'd only get jealous anyway.

The e-mail after that made Madison laugh. With Mom's approval, she'd signed up online to receive a Go Nikki! Fan Club Newsletter. An e-mail announcement had arrived in her e-mailbox in html format, which meant that a giant photo of Nikki popped up onscreen the moment Madison opened up the mail. In the picture, Nikki looked perfect—no zits, no bad attitude, nothing wrong. Madison hit DELETE. Nikki wasn't that perfect. No one was.

As Madison moved along to the next e-mail, she laughed even harder than she had at the Nikki newsletter. As usual, Dad had sent along one of his lame-o jokes.

From: JeffFinn
To: MadFinn
Subject: Dinner?
Date: Fri 24 May 9:51 PM
Why did the FHJH Student put on mascara in math class?

Because she was taking a makeup exam!

So I'm here with Stephanie and we're thinking of you being at the concert. Wow. You have to call and tell me everything.

Let's have dinner Monday night instead? I already checked with your mother and she was fine with that.

Love, Dad

P.S. Did you know that it takes only 17 muscles to smile and 43 muscles to frown! I hope you're smiling right now!

Madison skim-read the e-mails from her BFFs next. They had written first thing that morning to say that the concert had been the best night in their entire lives. Madison wrote back "TOTALLY!" They agreed to meet up later that Saturday for ice cream at Freeze Palace or maybe to rent a movie over at Aimee's house. Attached to Aimee's e-mail was a link to the Web site of her dance school. She wanted Madison and Fiona both to see the program for her upcoming recital. "I can dance better than Nikki! LOL!" Aimee wrote.

The last remaining e-mail in the box was the one

Madison was most excited to open and read. Hearing from her best friends was always fun, but getting keypal mail was super special. It made Madison feel important. And she always knew the right things to say.

Unlike Madison, Bigwheels had obviously gotten up early in Washington, which was three hours behind Far Hills. She'd just sent the e-mail a little while before Madison opened it.

```
From: Bigwheels
To: MadFinn
Subject: Write Back Soon
Date: Sat 25 May 10:04 AM
```
I can't sleep late anymore on weekends because my little sister has to go to this special accelerated class on Saturdays. Mom makes us rise and shine at the crack of dawn. But at least I can write to you! That and watch cartoons. They are showing this bonanza of old Bugs 'Bunny cartoons and they make me laugh so hard. I also love the Powerpuff Girls even though my uncool sister does too.

HOW WAS THE CONCERT????!!! I have been thinking about you since yesterday. I told my mom that I wanted to go to the Nikki show and she said "NO WAY," so all the more reason why I wish I were you. Was she amazing? I think that she wears the best clothes. I saw on one of her Web sites that the theme of her concert is like a carnival or something. Is that true?

Send me ur update. I will be waiting!

Yours till the flower pots,

Bigwheels a/k/a Victoria a/k/a Vicki

p.s. That's what most people call me at school and I don't think I told you that—Vicki. CWYL! Bye!

Madison dashed off an extra long e-mail. She included all the details too, right down to Ivy's appearance and Nikki's zits.

The rest of Saturday flew by. And Sunday, too. Madison spring cleaned her closet with Mom's help, boxing up some of her winter sweaters to put upstairs in the attic. Spring was here, and summer wasn't too far off.

By Monday morning, the high of the concert had mostly worn off, although everyone in school was talking about Nikki. Most people were still idolizing her clothes and her poses, but Madison and her friends knew something everyone else didn't. Before homeroom, Madison went into her school locker and peeled off the Nikki poster from the door. She didn't worship the singing star quite as much as she had a few days before.

"I still can't believe we met her. In person!" Aimee said. "She wasn't that bad, was she?"

"She was kind of rude to you," Fiona reminded Aimee. "Don't you remember?"

"I want to put a picture of you guys up on my locker instead," Madison said.

Aimee threw her arms into the air. "Oh yeah, because we are just soooo much more beautiful!"

Madison smiled. "Well, we're not famous. But so what?"

"Do either of you have a math quiz today? Can I borrow someone's notes?" Fiona asked. "Since the Nikki concert happened, I didn't concentrate on any-thing else. I have so much homework and studying to make up!"

Madison was about to commiserate with her BFF, when someone called out to her from across the hallway.

"Hey, Finnster!"

It was Hart Jones. As soon as Madison heard his voice, she turned away. She was trying hard to ignore him. But then he walked by and all hope was lost. As soon as she laid eyes on his brown curly hair, Madison's heart began to pitter and pat. She said a soft "Hello," and he smiled.

As soon as the class bell rang, the three friends went their separate ways. Madison spent the morning classes in a little bit of a post-concert fog. She'd had the whole weekend to recover, and she'd torn the locker poster down, but Madison was still thinking about Nikki.

On the way to lunch that afternoon, Madison passed through the school's main lobby. A small group of kids had gathered in front of the display case in the center of the lobby. As Madison drew closer to the glass cabinet, she saw that Mr. Duane had put up an art exhibit.

Madison Finn's self-portrait was in the middle of everything.

"That looks really good," a voice said from behind her.

Madison spun around to see who was talking.

It was Carmen.

"I like the way your self-portrait is kind of abstract. It's way better than everyone else's," Carmen said. "More interesting."

Madison wasn't so sure "interesting" was a good thing.

"Thanks," she mumbled, slinging her orange bag over her shoulder. "I guess it's okay—if you like blobs."

"Mr. Duane wouldn't have put yours in the middle if he didn't like it, would he?" Carmen asked. She smiled, and Madison noticed again how pretty she was up close.

"I guess you're right," Madison said. She glanced around the cabinet so she could see Carmen's portrait, too. It was tacked up a row away.

"No one's picture really looks like them," Carmen observed.

"Yours does," Madison said. "You are such a good artist. I meant to say that in class the other day. I was really frustrated drawing that fruit."

"Thanks for saying that," Carmen said in a soft voice, smiling even wider.

"Well, I have to go to lunch now," Madison said. "What are you doing?"

"I have lunch, too," Carmen said. "Wanna sit together?"

Madison wondered what Fiona and Aimee would say if she brought a new friend over to the orange table at the back of the cafeteria. What would Hart Jones say if he saw Madison talking to Carmen? Did it matter?

She glanced back at her self-portrait one last time and heard another kid say something about how cool it looked.

Madison beamed.

Like her picture, she wasn't perfect either, but it didn't matter so much anymore.

"Let's go to lunch!" Madison said to Carmen, and they disappeared down the hall.

Mad Chat Words:

```
<:>))        Very, VERY happy
:-6          I'm sooo wiped out
&'''-1       You're making me cry!
RN!          Right now!
YTTT?        You're telling me the truth?
BFB          Bigfishbowl
2morrow      Tomorrow
Tix          Tickets
WWBY         Wouldn't Wanna Be You
WBS          Write back soon
GMTA         Great minds think alike
CWYL         Chat with you later
TX           Thanks
YW           You're welcome
```

Madison's Computer Tip

HELP! That seems to be my favorite word these days. Sometimes I really do need help, though . . . *fast*. **E-mails and IM's are a great way to reach out for help and advice from friends—and get answers fast.** Like when I asked Fiona for fashion advice for the Nikki concert and she gave it to me . . . presto . . . online! And I love the fact that I send e-mail to my keypal Bigwheels all the way across the country, and moments later she's giving me the best advice in the world.

Visit Madison at www.madisonfinn.com

Chicago together and then I'll go on to my business trip . . ."

Madison stood up and threw her arms into the air. "Are you kidding, Mom? Leave my friends to go hang with Gramma Helen? No way."

Mom nodded. "I know it doesn't sound perfect, but it will be just for a week or so. Gramma keeps saying how much she misses you and how she wants to see you."

"A WEEK?" Madison said. She leaned back in the swing seat and sighed a deep, sad sigh.

No Far Hills carnival? No parade? She'd miss the fireworks?

She'd miss her friends.

Mom and Madison sat there not speaking for a moment or two. There was total silence except for the sound of Phin's panting.

"Maddie," Mom finally said. "This doesn't have to be a tragedy."

"Easy for you to say," Madison groaned. She felt like crying and screaming at the same time. The Fourth of July was her big chance to hang out with Hart Jones. Now those hopes were dashed.

Phinnie started to howl a little, like he knew something was wrong. He sniffed at Madison's sneakers.

"Rowrrooooooo!"

"I really am sorry, Maddie," Mom said again. She rubbed the top of Madison's back like she always did when Madison felt sad or sick.

"Like when?" Madison asked.

"Well . . . around the Fourth of July," Mom replied. "It's bad timing, I know . . ."

"Bad timing? IT'S AWFUL!" Madison blurted, her face swelling up pink. "I can't miss the Fourth of July."

"Maddie . . . honey bear . . ." Mom said, reaching out for Madison's arm; but Madison pulled away.

"Just because you have work, why do I have to leave, too? When were you going to tell me? Can I at least stay with Daddy?" Madison asked three questions all at once.

Mom shook her head. "No, I checked—and your father has a business commitment on the other coast that he can't avoid. And I asked Aimee's mom if you could sleep over with them, but they have several guests coming from out of town, too. Oh, Maddie, it's just one of those things. I'm sorry."

Madison's face was all puffy.

"You don't understand, Mom," Madison said. Her knees locked and the swing stopped. "This is the most important Fourth of July ever . . . in my whole entire life. I can't miss it."

"I'm sorry, Maddie. But we'll make other arrangements. . . ." Mom's voice drifted off.

"What *kind* of arrangements?" Madison asked.

Mom put her hand on Madison's back. "I think you should go to Gramma Helen's for the Fourth of July. And she loves the idea. We can fly out to

3

"Oh, I don't know. You haven't seen them in a few days and . . . well, I just don't want this to be a summer of you sleeping late and staying inside on the computer all day—"

"Mom," Madison said, interrupting. "What are you talking about? I get out. I walk Phinnie. I've been over to the animal clinic—"

"*Once,*" Mom cut her off. "Now, we just went and bought you that nice new swimsuit. I think you should use it. Isn't there some lake party coming up? Should we have made camp plans for you?"

Madison made a grouchy face. Ever since the Big D, her parents divorce, Mom was overly worried about everything Madison did and did not do.

"I'm super-fine the way I am," Madison said. "Besides, the Fourth of July is coming up, and we're going to help the Parks Department with the setup. They ask for junior high volunteers. That way we all see fireworks up close."

"Well," Mom continued. "We need to talk about the Fourth of July."

Silently, Madison dragged her feet along the ground so the swing moved back and forth. She had a sneaking suspicion that she did not want to hear the next part of what Mom had to say.

Mom kept talking. "Unfortunately, I have to work on an important business presentation next week—and then I have to fly out and present it—"

2

Take a sneak peek at the new

From the Files of

Madison Finn

#9: Just Visiting

Chapter 1

On the Finn porch, Mom had installed a wooden swing seat, and Madison collapsed into its puffy blue cushions. Their house had a western view, so she leaned backward to see if the sun might set while she waited. The whole sky was turning a washed-out yellow, but summer dusk was hours away.

After a few moments, Mom came outside and sat down beside her.

"Did you see Aimee and Fiona today?" Mom asked.

"Nah, but we talked on the phone. Why?" Madison asked back.